*"Tell me what you [want,]
Melissa."*

Melissa took a deep breath. "I...I want to try new things. I want an adventure. Something I can remember when I'm fifty and I've been with the same guy for twenty years. I want anything and everything but the same old missionary grind."

Riley slid his hands up her thighs to her waist. "I understand," he murmured, tightening his hold into a strong, reassuring grip.

She pressed herself against him, shocked to feel him hard between them. *Oh, man. He wants me. A guy like this...*

He led her over to the couch and pulled her down across his lap, kissing her all the while. She sank against him, totally carried away by the man and his mouth. Then his hands came up under her skirt, skimmed her thighs and settled on the mound of her sex through her panties.

Arousal seared through her; she gasped and arched up instinctively for more pressure, shocked by his boldness, shocked by her own. She'd never been this hot, this ready....

If he touched her, she'd die. If he didn't, she'd die faster.

Blaze™

Dear Reader,

Harlequin Blaze is a supersexy new series. If you like love stories with a strong sexual edge then this is the line for you! The books are fun and flirtatious, the heroes are hot and outrageous. Blaze is a series for the woman who wants *more* in her reading pleasure....

This month bestselling Harlequin Presents author Miranda Lee delivers #9 *Just a Little Sex...* about one night of passion that turns into much more! Rising star Jamie Denton says you need to break the rules in #10 *Sleeping With the Enemy,* a story with sizzling sexual tension and erotic love scenes. Talented Isabel Sharpe takes us to #11 *The Wild Side,* a fun, lusty tale about a good girl who decides bad might be better. Popular Janelle Denison rounds out the month with #12 *Heat Waves,* another SEXY CITY NIGHTS story set in fiery Chicago—where the heat definitely escalates after dark....

Look for four Blaze books every month at your favorite bookstore. And check us out online at eHarlequin.com and tryblaze.com.

Enjoy!

Birgit Davis-Todd
Senior Editor & Editorial Coordinator
Harlequin Blaze

THE WILD SIDE

Isabel Sharpe

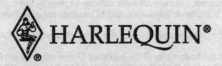

HARLEQUIN®

TORONTO • NEW YORK • LONDON
AMSTERDAM • PARIS • SYDNEY • HAMBURG
STOCKHOLM • ATHENS • TOKYO • MILAN • MADRID
PRAGUE • WARSAW • BUDAPEST • AUCKLAND

To Barbara, Elizabeth, Heather, Karen and Susie,
who deserve public recognition for twenty-plus years
listening to my sorrows, laughing at my jokes
and tolerating my neuroses as only the best friends do.

ISBN 0-373-79015-5

THE WILD SIDE

Copyright © 2001 by Muna Shehadi Sill.

This edition published by arrangement with Harlequin Books S.A.

Visit us at www.eHarlequin.com

Printed in U.S.A.

A NOTE FROM THE AUTHOR...

I've always preferred Mr. Personality to dark brooding hunks. Guys with whom I could imagine enjoying morning-after conversation almost as much as how we spent the previous evening. This is one of the reasons I love writing for Harlequin Duets, which is where you may have met me before.

But...to my surprise, I absolutely loved writing Riley, the darkest, broodingest, hunkiest hero I've ever created. I had a blast messing up his precise, controlled life by assigning him Melissa, whose natural humor, quirky cynicism and frank desire for sexual experimentation rattle him in a way he's not at all prepared for.

Throw in stolen jewelled art, a little suspense and a secondary couple who have an equally rocky journey to love, and you've taken a walk with me on *The Wild Side*.

Enjoy!

Isabel Sharpe

P.S. I love hearing from readers. Write to me at IsaSharpe@aol.com.

Prologue

ROSE BLEW HER NOSE, then added the tissue to the pile on her pink-and-white rose-print bedspread. She glanced at the clock and collapsed into another spasm of sobbing. It was 9:00 a.m. Half an hour since the tears had started. This bout should be wrapping up pretty soon.

She'd finally gotten to where she could view her crying fits philosophically. Months could go by without them, but sooner or later, one would catch up with her. Put them down to exhaustion, maybe mild depression, hormones…whatever.

At first she'd thought she was going crazy. Now she considered the tears a harmless and probably healthy form of stress relief. Since her apartment had been broken into, the crying jags had been coming more frequently. Little wonder. That sense of unease, of her privacy being violated, had lingered, as if the intruder were still hiding in her home.

Ten minutes later, the sobs subsided into shuddering sighs, then hiccups. Rose blew her nose again and gathered up the tissues to take to the trash, giving one last sigh—of relief this time. She crossed to the window, over the colorful rugs strewn on her hardwood floor, wincing when she put weight on the foot His Royal Majesty, Prince Rajid of Saudi Arabia, had stepped on last night. Sweet guy. Rotten dancer.

But then they all had some flaw, fatal or otherwise—not that she had perfection sewn up by any means. Deep down she suspected the man didn't exist who could make her fall so far in love she'd forsake all others. Though on some level, however shallow, she did love all the men she dated, from the bottoms of their feet to the tops of their enormous, fragile egos. She loved how they looked at her, how they made her feel. Loved the power she had to entice or amuse or excite them. The only thing she'd ever really been good at. Like an alcoholic or a smoker, she was addicted. To men.

But real take-over-your-soul love? She doubted she was capable of it. Her personal fatal flaw, perhaps.

Rose wiped away the last tear from her cheek and drew aside the white lace curtain to see if the van across the street was still parked there. Before the break-in and before that horrible threatening letter, her addiction had seemed harmless. She got everything she wanted. The men got *most* of what they wanted. Now someone wanted more from her than a good time. And she hadn't a clue who it was or what it was all about. Someone stalking her? An angry ex-beau? A few men had protested when she'd ended their relationship, but most had parted on friendly terms and gone off on their next hunt.

Maybe it was something in the apartment. She'd gotten plenty of gifts over the years. Maybe some guy had given her heirloom jewelry by mistake and Mama wanted it back.

She could only hope it was that easy.

The van sat across Garden Street, as usual. Ted's TV Repair. She shivered and swallowed more threatening tears. Call her paranoid, but she couldn't shake the feeling that someone was watching her from that van. She ought to call the police and ask them to check it out. Of course, it could *be* the police, keeping close tabs since the break-in. Either way, police or criminal, Rose felt threatened, claustrophobic.

So much for her Total Relaxation Saturdays.

Her phone rang; she jumped and pulled her bathrobe more tightly around her. People she loved knew Saturday was her no-phone, vegging day. The day she always refused invitations, in some perverse homage to the dateless Saturdays she'd suffered in high school. It was her day to sit home in her pajamas with the frogs on them, watch bad TV, eat chocolate, write letters the nurses could read to her mom.... Her day of regression. No social responsibilities. No cleaning. No makeup. No men.

The machine picked up the call. Clicked. Clicked again. Senator Alvin Mason's patrician voice played on the tape. "Come on, Rose. I know you're there. Pick up. It's important."

Rose's brows drew down. He sounded strange... strained. Unusual for Mr. Hearty-Sound-Bite. They'd dated for a few months, a year or so ago, before he decided he'd have more political success as a married man, and had gone hunting for a suitable wife.

She picked up. "I'm here."

"How are you, Rose?"

Rose frowned. He didn't sound like he gave a rat's ass how she felt. And she could have sworn she heard a truck go by in the background. Was one of Massachusetts's most illustrious politicians calling from a pay phone? "I'm okay. You sound horrible. Where are you calling fr—"

"I heard about the break-in." He nearly shouted to be heard over another engine. "They didn't take anything."

"No." She wrapped the phone cord around a tight fist. How did he know that? "I got a letter, too, two days ago. Telling me to watch out."

Massachusetts's Senator-for-the-Wholesome-Family swore obscenely. For one sweet moment, Rose allowed herself to feel pleasure at his protectiveness. Then scoffed at her own Cinderella-bullcrap mentality.

"This wasn't supposed to—" He swore again.

Rose held absolutely still. The phone cord swayed gently against the wooden end table her great-great-grandmother had brought over from England. *Oh, God. He was part of it.* "You know something about this?"

She barely recognized her own voice. Not the sweet, sexy girl everyone thought she was, but harsh, hard-edged. A grown woman afraid for her life.

The senator took a deep breath, audible even over the traffic noise. "Rose…"

She closed her eyes; her body began to shake.

"Rose…" His voice was quiet, calm, deadly serious. "I think you should go away for a while."

1

RILEY ANDERSON LOWERED himself into the grimy booth opposite Charlie Watson, captain in the Boston Police Force and primary supporter of the city's greasy spoon establishments. Hands folded on the table, Riley greeted him and sat straight, regarding Watson evenly so as not to betray either interest or suspicion. Cops didn't summon private investigators to out-of-the-way burger joints unless they were in deep.

"Thing is…" Watson tossed back the last French fry and looked wistfully at his empty plate. "Thing is, I wouldn't come to you unless it was an absolute last resort. We've got plenty of people on the force who could handle this."

Riley nodded, not rising to the bait, not moving, though the booth hit his back in uncomfortable places. Holding still and watching went a long way toward making people reveal things they weren't planning to—if they were hiding anything in the first place. The jury was still out on the captain.

Watson took a gulp of soda from a gargantuan cup and plopped it down in what he probably thought was a powerful gesture. He narrowed his eyes, which were an incongruous shade of ice-blue against his pale, flabby face. "Truth is, we have a situation. Involving important people. Very important. Another situation at the station. Very bad. I can't risk—"

"Captain." Riley lifted one eyebrow a fraction, all he'd allow to show of his impatience. "The point. Get to it."

Watson crushed a burger wrapper and tossed it onto his tray, pale eyes never leaving Riley's face. "Okay, you want it straight? I'll give it to you straight. I don't like having to come to you—don't like it at all. But we got a leak at the station. Someone has developed a big mouth, and his big mouth is jeopardizing the investigation. I can't trust anyone. You, I trust. I don't like you, but I trust you."

Riley nodded. He didn't like *or* trust Charlie Watson, but now was probably not the best time to say so. "What's the job?"

"It involves the apartment of a certain woman named Rose. Just Rose. Like Cher is just Cher." He pushed back a few combed-over strands of hair that had broken free of whatever glue he used to hold them in place. "We think she might have received stolen property, possibly unwittingly. Property we are anxious to return to…the previous owners. She reported a break-in recently, nothing taken. Someone knows or suspects she's got the goods. We're watching the place in case someone makes another move, but I don't want my detectives poking around until I know who I can trust."

Riley clenched his teeth. Getting information out of the captain was like playing twenty questions. He leaned forward and fixed Watson with an even stare. "What would I be looking for?"

"Art." The captain groped in his pocket and came up with a roll of antacids, avoiding Riley's eyes. "An antique miniature portrait. Jeweled frame. Supposed to be worth a ton, what the hell do I know about it?

But it's more than that. We want you to be Rose's special new friend, and figure out what the hell she knows.''

Riley relaxed his jaw, willing himself to be patient. "Who is Rose and where does she fit?"

Watson looked around, as if the elderly couple on one side and the frazzled mom with four kids on the other could be undercover agents. He propped his elbows on the table, hefted his bulk forward and beckoned Riley closer. "Here's the thing. She's supposed to be a total babe. Different guy every night. You know the type. We talked to some of the guys she used to date. Get this. They all had a completely different description of her: clothes, hair, eye color, even personality. But definitely the same Rose. This chick completely reinvents herself for whatever man she's with. Can you beat that? Dates 'em for a while, they go nuts over her, shower her with gifts, then she's on to the next one. When she reported the break-in, she had my toughest detective whipped in about ten minutes. Some operator.''

Watson blew out an admiring whistle that grated on Riley's nerves. What the hell was there to admire in a woman like that? "So some smitten sop gave her the portrait for her personal enrichment.''

"Ha! Not likely." Watson slapped his fist on his thigh, obviously missing Riley's sarcasm. "His *physical* enrichment, more like it.''

Riley compressed his lips, which wanted to curl in disgust. Just the type of woman you'd like to bring home to Mom for Sunday dinner. But the case intrigued him for some reason he couldn't quite pin down. Watson knew a hell of a lot more than he was telling. "Who were the previous owners of the portrait?"

"That's where I cut you off, Anderson." Watson's eyes narrowed into puffy slits. "This is police business. You get into her place and find the portrait. Report back to me on your progress. Don't call the station, don't talk to anyone else about this. If word got out among my men that you're involved I'd have a mutiny."

Riley nodded, blood pumping. This case had to be about more than wealthy art lovers wanting their precious portrait back. He wanted in.

He moved his jaw to fight back a grin. Slate would love it. Riley's comrade-in-arms, partner and best friend was currently at the family cottage on the coast of Maine, mourning his mother's death from cancer.

Riley and Slate had been a successful, and eventually highly decorated, Marine Recon fighting unit that had earned the respect of their peers and commanders alike. Gemini. The twins. In the field they'd developed such a bond that they barely needed to speak when they went on missions. If Riley's instincts proved correct, and he'd need to do some digging to see, this case might induce Slate to return to civilization after the long year spent nursing his mom. It had been too long since they'd worked together.

Riley nodded again at Watson. "I'll do it."

"Not a tough assignment. I'm guessing the way you look, you won't have any trouble getting friendly with this Rose character." Watson sniggered and tipped back his soda cup, then cursed as an avalanche of crushed ice spilled onto his face and shirt.

Riley allowed himself a faint smile. If only justice got meted out so quickly all the time.

He stayed at the restaurant just long enough to agree on terms, preferring fresh air to deep-fat-fryer fumes, and preferring nearly anyone to Charlie Watson for company. Then he pushed open the bell-jangling door and headed for Cambridge street, inhaling the warm late-June air. Tourists flocked among the pigeons on City Hall Plaza; the breeze in his face brought the faint tang of the sea from nearby Boston Harbor. Riley headed for the Government Center T stop. Might as well take a look at this Rose woman's apartment building this afternoon. Check out the scene, formulate a plan, then do some digging. Send Slate a telegram if he uncovered anything worthwhile.

The unmistakable nerve-burning sensation of being watched made him hesitate in his stride for a fraction of a second. He waited until he came opposite the low brick wall surrounding the entrance to the T, then turned, keeping the wall at his back.

A man. Clean-cut. Nice suit. Bulge for the gun. Government agent.

Riley set his feet slightly apart, hands at his waist and expression neutral as the man approached. His instincts had proved correct earlier than he'd anticipated. Coming so soon on the heels of the bizarre summons from Watson, this could mean only one thing. Whatever this guy wanted had something to do with Rose the Man-eater and her art collector boyfriend.

"Ted Barker, FBI." The man flashed a government credential from his wallet. "And you are Riley Anderson, private investigator, ex-Marine Force Recon, half of Gemini."

"Yes." Riley met the man's eyes impassively, surprised to see what looked like a trace of admiration and respect in the FBI regulation sneer. "What can I do for you?"

"We'd like to talk to you." Ted Barker, FBI, put away his ID and gestured to the black Lincoln Towne Car across the street. "We think you can help us."

"Wow." Melissa Rogers widened her eyes and leaned forward on the living room sofa in her Cambridge apartment, over the bowl of popcorn clutched in her lap. "Oh, wow."

On her television screen, halfway through the movie *9 1/2 Weeks,* a blindfolded Kim Basinger lay on her back in an open white shirt and white bikini panties, cigarette smoke swirling behind her in the blue-white light of a desk lamp. Mickey Rourke, smirking in devilish black, fished an ice cube out of his drink and held it for a camera close-up. Cold wet drips fell into Kim's mouth, trickled between her lips, down her breasts, hardened her nipples, rolled into her navel.

"Oh, oh, wow. Look at how he...oh, wow."

Her friend Penny grabbed a handful of popcorn from her own bowl and turned to Melissa in irritation. "Will you stop with the 'Oh wow' and let me watch the movie? You're ruining it."

Melissa forced her mouth shut, except when it needed to admit another influx of popcorn. And except when Kim was sitting on the floor in Mickey's kitchen, eyes closed while he fed her—strawberries, cherries, olives, champagne—then squirted honey on her outstretched tongue, and onto her chin, and knees, and legs; used his hands to spread the sticky golden fluid around her thighs, around and in, and up, and higher....

Melissa opened her mouth and formed the words silently. *Oh, wow.*

The movie spun on, ended; credits rolled up the screen. A strange, almost angry longing charged through Melissa's body. She smacked her fist on her sensible dark beige, Scotchgarded couch. "Why can't something like that happen to me?"

"What." Penny screwed up her face incredulously. "You want to meet a controlling, sadistic psycho who almost ruins your life?"

"No, no, no." Melissa pushed the popcorn off her lap and stretched her bare feet rigidly out in front of her, trying to calm the emotional need for physical action. "I mean I want that kind of excitement, that danger. I want to be swept away by passion, even if it's not sensible. Maybe especially because it isn't sensible."

"You and the entire population since man walked upright. Get real, Melissa. It don't happen. By the time you get to sex, you and Mr. Whoever know too much about each other. There's always baggage, always a power play, or at the very least you start worrying that your thighs feel too squishy, your arm is in the way or you're taking too long to come and he'll get impatient." She pushed her oblong wire rims higher up on her nose. "Swept away by passion is for the movies. Trust me."

"What about sex with a guy you don't know? Someone you don't have baggage with yet?" Melissa blurted the words out, shocked she'd admit considering such a thing, even to her best friend. Some hungry demon had recently invaded her personality and begun gobbling up her common sense.

"Huh? You want to risk messing sheets with a guy who turns out to be Mr. Diseased Serial-Killer?"

"Okay, look. I want a deep, meaningful relationship as much as anyone else. I want to get married someday, and I know the kind of guy that can make me happy. But marriage is like life was for the five years I dated Bill. Comfortable intimacy, predictable dates, same old fights about the same old issues." Melissa gestured in the air and let her hand flop disgustedly into her lap. "I understand that. I don't expect it to be a rest-of-my-life thrill. But I'm not married now. I want something different, a totally shallow and exciting and fabulous adventure with someone I know is completely wrong for me."

Penny snapped her wide-open mouth shut. "Since when have you been Ms. Hot-to-Trot?"

Melissa sat up and curled her legs under her. "I don't know. I'm tired of being sensible and dependable and predictable. I want to try being someone else for a change."

Penny rolled her eyes. "Who, Mata Hari?"

"Why not?" Melissa stretched her arms over her head and grinned. "After all those years with Bill, and then the months of misery after he dumped me, I feel alive. Like I've been asleep all my life and I'm just waking up."

Penny peered over the tops of her glasses, brows raised. "Today is the first day of the rest of your life?"

Melissa grabbed a handful of popcorn and lobbed it at her friend. "Many thanks for taking my late-twenties crisis so seriously."

"Aw, hon, you know I care. I just think sex is not any kind of a cure for what ails you."

"Then what is?"

"Love." Penny nodded emphatically. "You need to fall in love."

"Oh, please. I was in love with Bill. Look where that got me."

"Ha! Bill was a habit, not love. Give yourself some time. Look around. Ask your friends. Not me, though. If I knew an adorable, single, straight guy I wouldn't let you near him." Penny heaved her well-padded self up to her full five-foot-two-inch height, shook off the popcorn in a gentle rain onto Melissa's hardwood floor and scooped it back into her empty bowl. "Me, I must go. I have to be at the museum shop early tomorrow. We're expecting a huge shipment of mini *Thinker* statues for the Rodin exhibit."

Melissa saw her friend to the door and waved goodbye, then lingered in the hallway, listening to the giggles and booming laughter coming from the apartment across the hall. Rose must have brought her date home tonight. The woman never stopped.

Again that strange, wild yearning slammed into Melissa. Sort of a combination of lust, fury and panic. Like she'd been trapped in a tiny elevator with John Cusack and didn't know whether to jump him, force back the doors with Superwoman strength or freak from claustrophobia.

The door to Rose's apartment opened. Melissa stepped back and guiltily gave in to her voyeuristic mood by closing her door most of the way and gluing her eye to the crack.

A dark-skinned, tuxedoed man, probably once gorgeous, now handsome in a balding, middle-aged kind of way, emerged, pulling a laughing young woman behind him. Melissa's eyes stretched wide. Rose looked like something out of a 1940s movie tonight. Her hair, undoubtedly a wig, fell carefully around her face in dark waves. She wore an unusually modest, rose-colored gown that showed off her fair skin, nipped in her already tiny waist and flowed down to a stunning floor-length skirt. Tonight, instead of the sultry pout she'd had on for her last date she glowed with girlish enthusiasm.

Every time a different man. Every time a new look.

Melissa's body contracted with fierce longing. She wanted that. That ability to try out a new personality, to let loose, experiment, play. Just for a month or two. More than that and she'd get sick of it, for sure. But two months of wild, nonstop partying and blow-me-away passion would be fine.

The man swept Rose into an embrace and pushed her back against the wall, kissed her mouth, face and hands, and then ruined the entire mood by making a doggy growling noise deep in his throat. Melissa made a gagging face and closed the door noiselessly on Rose's pretend-outrage squeal of "Oh, Your *Majesty.*"

Ix-nay on the oggies-day. Melissa didn't need a "Your Majesty," either. She wasn't that picky, by any means. Just a nice parade of your garden-variety perfect studs who could go all night.

She slumped back onto her couch. Who was she kidding? A different man every night? Ick. But *one* would be great. One no-strings man who set her clock ticking, with whom she could explore things Bill had never shown her. One man who would do a damn sight more than climb on top of her, produce a lot of noise and sweat, then roll off, mumble an endearment or two and start snoring. Maybe someone tremendously talented with ice cubes and honey.

She looked down at her bare feet, ratty shorts and *Toy Story* T-shirt and pushed back her straight, bobbed hair self-consciously. *Yeah, right.* She was sex goddess material for sure. Men would throng to her door the minute she announced herself available. An entire squadron of supergeeks, fresh from their *Star Trek* convention. A brood of wholesome innocents brought up lusting after Mary Ann on *Gilligan's Island* instead of Ginger.

Hardly the beefcake she had in mind. But the really amazing guys never gave her a second glance. She was always the cute little sister they never had.

Aw...

Melissa sneered and threw a newly recovered brown couch pillow across the room. Fine. She'd been toying with the idea of a makeover for years, but Bill always insisted she'd look fake.

Well, tough. Bill was history. The time was right. If Rose could reinvent herself, so could Melissa. Not for nothing was she assistant director of marketing at the Museum of Fine Arts. Her job was to make things sexy that people might not think were sexy otherwise. If she could make 'em line up around the block for a glimpse of shards from an ancient Egyptian cooking pot, she could make herself over into the kind of woman someone other than Elmer Fudd would find attractive. Right?

Right.

She grabbed the July issue of *Cosmo* off her coffee table and leafed through, noting the styles and attitudes of the models. Where to begin? If she was going to go on a rampage, even if she ended up doing so only mentally—an attitude change if not a real sexual odyssey—then she'd have to make sure she got a style she could live with. She stopped and stabbed her finger on the picture of a sleek pouty model with a cap of dark hair. Her all-black, figure-hugging outfit made her look casual, elegant, sexy and innocent all at once, exactly what Melissa wanted.

She shut the magazine and hugged it to her chest. The works. The whole shebang. The New Her. To celebrate her final thrilling freedom from loving Bill. To celebrate the need to explore that strange dark desire that had been thrashing around inside her for the past few weeks. To celebrate the birth of her female power and the chance to bring it to its fullest, most independent potential.

Now just one problem. Where was she going to find the man? The one who'd do all this investigating with her? Help explore the depth of her femininity? Help her overcome any and all inhibitions and take her places she'd never—

"Oh, *yes,* Your Majesty!" Rose's voice carried clearly from the corridor right into Melissa's fantasy.

Melissa smiled. Right on cue, not that she would have taken long to think of Rose. What more could she ask for? The new Melissa was a done deal. She had the desire, the means—and the perfect mentor right across the hall.

2

MICHAEL SLATER TOOK a deep breath of the sea breeze wafting through the screened-in porch of his parents' summer house in Howarth, Maine. Below him, sparkling through the evergreen branches and birch trunks, spread Fischer Bay, dotted with islands glowing green in the early sun. The still-chilly morning air, spiced with the scent of pine and the sea, flowed over him with a cleansing freshness that went a long way toward instilling peace in his always-restless soul. The place definitely got under your skin, into your blood.

He took a few steps toward the south edge of the porch, running his hand along the screen, wet from last night's rain, causing a shower of drops to fall on his bare forearm. During the year he'd spent nursing his mother, he'd begun to appreciate solitude, something he'd never thought would happen after thirty-three years jammed with people.

But not *this* much solitude.

He clenched his fist; muscles contracted in his forearm, rolling away the drops of water collected from the screen. Since his energies had stopped being focused on keeping his mother alive, keeping her comfortable, he'd started wanting someone around. Maybe Riley would want to visit. He missed Riley. Maybe a woman. He damn well missed women. He could see a woman here, in this idyllic place, moving around the house, reading on the porch or sitting on the rocky shore watching the water.

He laughed; the sound startled a hummingbird hovering at a nearby tree. Maybe he should pack up and go back to Boston, back to telephones and electricity and cynical city dwellers before he turned into a total sap.

Sounds that had grown unfamiliar broke the tranquil morning behind him in the woods. A rough engine, a truck or a van, crunching stones on the dirt road, pinging them out of the way of its wheels. Slate swung around, staring apprehensively through the house toward the front entrance. Who the hell would be coming at this time of morning?

The bell rang twice, impatiently. He went to the door, grimacing at the intrusion into his day.

A pimply, long-haired kid moved his head in rhythm to whatever horrible music was blaring through his headphones directly into his eardrums. "Telegram. Sign here, please."

Slate quelled a flash of alarm, signed the form and took the telegram into the house, breathing in relief when the noise of the van engine faded away. He went back out onto the porch and opened the envelope slowly, carefully. Then stared, adrenaline making his body taut.

Just one word: *Gemini.*

MELISSA SAT ON THE EDGE of her bed in unfamiliar tight black pants, an olive-green tank top and chunky shoes, staring at the Brand-New Her in the mirror. Her straight bob had given way to a short cut that outlined the shape of her face and head and made her eyes look enormous. And lo and behold, freed from the weight of its former length, her hair had actually managed to wave slightly, though it did better on humid days.

After the haircut—miraculously, she'd gotten the appointment two days after she decided on her new look—she'd gone on to take a free makeup lesson at a department store counter, and emerged looking like some Bride of Dracula who had never seen the sun. Pale powdery skin, dark lips, orangey blush in places she never blushed. Layers of eye shadow in progressively lighter shades, which was supposed to make her eyes look "natural," but which changed their shape so that she scarcely recognized herself... It had been a horror.

So she and Penny had invaded the makeup aisle at Walgreen's and spent an extended evening with *Cosmo* as their guide, trying to see if their fresh-faced farm-girl features could be coaxed into exotic sensual splendor.

Okay, well, they got close enough.

Then there was the manicure, and the pedicure, and the rather painful waxing, which did leave her legs fabulously smooth after the welts died down.

Melissa smiled at herself in the dark-framed mirror on her dresser. She did look different. Older. More sophisticated. Better. Up until now, it had been easy—a fun week. But now it was going to get harder, and scary. Now she was going to go over to Rose's apartment and ask how to meet a man she could have a wild, meaningless fling with. It was like the research was all finished, and now she had to sit down and write the term paper.

She curled her lip. So far she'd made it to the side

of her bed closest to the door. The next step would be walking out into her living room. From there, it was a matter of, say, fifteen feet to the front door. Six more to cross the hall. Then the knocking, the waiting, the small talk, and finally, Getting to the Point.

She shook her head in a quick shudder of denial. Insurmountable. She couldn't do it. Or maybe she could. But maybe tomorrow would be a better—

The phone rang next to her bed. She reached over her ivory bedspread and picked it up eagerly, hoping it was Penny, who would convince her tomorrow was a *much* better option. Or maybe one of her college roommates, who would talk to her until it was too close to dinner to go over there, or maybe—

"Melissa, it's Bill."

"Bill." Her way-over-him heart gave a traitorous flip. Was this a sign? A sign she was barking up the wrong tree entirely? "How...how are you doing?"

"I'm fine. Fine." He was distracted, uneasy. He had something to say. She knew without seeing him that he was puckering his mouth and drumming his fingers impossibly fast on whatever surface he was near. "How are *you* doing?"

"I'm great.... What's up?" Did he miss her? Did he want to see her? Did he want to get back together?

Forget it. Ha! She'd just tell him—

"I wanted to tell you..." He gave an exasperated sigh. "Maybe this was a stupid mistake. But I thought you should know."

"Yes?" *That I've been dreaming of you every night, Melissa. That I miss you more than I can say.*

Oh? Sorry, Bill. Life without you is just peachy. In fact, I'm about to—

"I met someone. I'm seeing someone. I...wanted you to hear it from me."

Melissa clenched her teeth in a huge happy smile and pasted her eyes open extra super-by-gosh wide. "Oh! Bill that's *fabulous!* I'm really happy for you. And *thanks* for telling me. That was so *sweet* of you!"

"Oh, man, I'm so glad you're not upset. She's pretty terrific." He gave a gooey chuckle. "Hey! Maybe you could come over sometime and meet—"

"Bill, thanks so much for calling. Great to hear from you. Gotta go. Bye."

Melissa hung up the phone, clenched her fists at her sides and punished her cool gray carpet with angry strides to the mirror, chest heaving from rage and hurt and humiliation and whatever else she could possibly be feeling. What bizarre, illogical trait made her want Bill to still want her just so she could have the luxury of disappointing him? So she could sit on her satin pillow, bejeweled and perfumed, smile indulgently and wave her silk hanky to the guards to drag him off to her castle's Rejected Males Room?

The minute he'd made it clear he didn't want her, her castle had turned into a scummy pond, and she was a princess reverting to frogdom, crouching on a cold slimy lily pad, lonely and hurt.

Well, to hell with him.

She turned abruptly and stalked through her apartment, swiped her keys off the hall table, banged through her door, took four furious steps down the corridor and knocked on Rose's door before she could weaken even slightly and change her mind.

"Who...who is it?"

Melissa frowned. Had she knocked that hard? Rose

sounded like she expected the entire Boston Police Force brandishing large weapons.

"It's Melissa. Can I talk to you?"

The door opened and Rose appeared, looking wan and uneasy and about five years younger than she had that night with the Saudi prince last week. She wore bright blue capris, and an oversize white shirt that probably used to belong to one of her male admirers.

"Sure. Sure." Rose smiled and beckoned. "Come on in. You look different. Did you change your hair? I like it. It looks kind of like mine."

Melissa nodded and touched her short hair self-consciously, unwilling to admit she'd had Rose's sleek, natural style in mind. Not that you saw much of Rose's hair since it was usually hiding under wigs.

"Would you like a cup of tea? I'm just making some."

Melissa nodded again and wandered among Rose's whimsical, colorful assortment of rugs, chairs and knickknacks, wondering what the etiquette was for asking someone she barely knew to recommend a sex partner. She picked up a hand mirror with the beautiful, delicate face of a girl painted on the back, and replaced it carefully on the cluttered coffee table.

"Lovely day." Rose smiled graciously. "I'm going to a Red Sox game tonight. Looks like we'll have good weather."

Come on, Melissa, spare her the small talk and get to the point. Melissa stopped opposite a bizarre giraffelike statue made out of tin cans wired together. "Oh, you have a Randstetler sculpture!"

"Is that what it is?" Rose rescued the shrieking kettle from its distress and poured boiling water into two cups. "A friend gave it to me. I can't say I love it."

"Your friend is very smart. Randstetler is starting to make a name for himself. His works will probably skyrocket in price. Strange guy, really into animal rights and kind of preachy about it. He works it into every subject." Melissa gently touched the giraffe's aluminum nose. *Okay. Enough prattle. Out with it.* "Listen, Rose. I wonder if I could ask you sort of a strange favor."

Rose laughed, a nice warm sound not at all like the silly giggle she'd been making in the hall with His Majesty. "I specialize in granting strange favors. And I was thinking of asking you for one, too. You first, though. Have a seat and ask away."

Melissa flopped into an overstuffed burgundy chair with a white lace antimacassar spread across the top. "I broke up with a guy a few months ago… Well, he broke up with me."

"Ugh." Rose wrinkled her nose, handed Melissa her tea and sank into a chair opposite. "I'm sorry."

"I'm fine. I'm fine now." Melissa set her mug carefully on a flowery coaster. "In fact, I'm ready to date again."

"Good for you."

"But I was wondering…well, the truth is, Bill and I…we didn't have the greatest sex life."

"Double ugh." Rose grimaced. "You're well rid of him."

"But before I start looking seriously… Since you seem to know so many guys, I was wondering…if you knew anyone I could have a fling with." Melissa covered her face with her hands. "Oh, man. If you knew how hard that was to come out with…"

"It's okay, it's okay." Rose laughed again. "I think it's a great idea. Everyone should have a wild romance or two."

Melissa dropped her hands. "Is that what you're doing?"

"Sort of." The friendly warmth in Rose's face dimmed. She took a sip of tea and brightened again. "Well, I'm happy to help. I do seem to know a lot of men."

"Oh, thank you." Melissa practically gasped out her relief. "I was so afraid you'd be offended."

Rose shook her head. "Nonsense. I admire you. I bet a lot of women want what you do, but don't have the courage to go after it."

"I don't feel courageous."

Rose shrugged. "What do they say in all the war movies? Courage is about acting brave when you're not feeling it."

"Thanks." Melissa grinned. For all her artifice around men, Rose was amazingly genuine.

"So, are you talking nice sweet gentle teacher? Or fulfilling your every fantasy with Mr. Studmuffins?"

"Mostly the latter." Melissa blushed, feeling as if she were discussing an order of meat at the supermarket. "I don't want to settle down until I've experienced some more of what everyone makes such a fuss about."

Rose smiled, a rueful Mona Lisa half smile. "You don't think a husband can give that to you?"

"Not what I'm after." Melissa swallowed some tea and shook her head emphatically. "Husbands come with the whole truckload of Having a Relationship. I want it free of the cargo this time, so I can try out being someone different, just for a while."

"I see." Rose put her tea down slowly. "Well, I'm hardly the one to talk you out of it. You're sure this is what you want? I mean, most women find it hard to…be intimate without falling in love."

"But you don't."

"No." Again the rueful smile. "I don't."

"Well, I won't know for sure until I try, but if I'm acting out a personality that isn't really me, and he's not the kind of average nice guy I usually go for, then I don't think the risk of real love is high." Melissa shrugged, stilling her hands, which had been twisting in her lap. "And if I get hurt, it's my fault. I asked for it."

"True." Rose sat quietly for a moment, then slapped her thigh. "So. If you're sure, I know I can help you."

"Oh. Wow. That's great." Melissa forced a smile, suddenly on the verge of panicking. What the hell did she expect? She was here because she knew Rose could help her.

Rose stood and went over to the window, glanced out rather anxiously, then perched on the sill. "I wonder if I could ask you a favor, too."

"Sure, of course."

"I need a place to…get away from it all for a while. I don't have much money, and I thought maybe if your family's condo in the Berkshires was free, you could…rent it to me cheap in exchange for Tom?"

Tom. The name shot a shiver through Melissa's body. *Oh, geez.* "I…don't see why not. My parents don't usually go up until mid-July. But I'd have to check with them."

"That would be great. I really need a vacation." Rose smiled, but her hands clenched the sill beneath her. "At any rate, Tom would be perfect. He's the friend of a friend—they may have dated briefly. Amanda can't say enough about him—handsome, sexy, gentle. One of those guys who's into women but not commitment. You'll probably like him."

"Oh. Wow. Okay." Melissa nodded rapidly, feeling like a complete fool.

Rose headed to the phone. "And if you don't, it's not like you have to do anything. I'll call Amanda for his number. Are you free tomorrow night?"

"Uh. Yes. I'm free." *Tomorrow?* Was she ready for this? Tomorrow? Did she really want to? This was totally terrifying.

Rose picked up the phone and dialed, smiling at Melissa. She chatted with Amanda and got Tom's number. Half fascinated, half freaking, Melissa gulped, feeling as if she'd run out of air and saliva at the same time. The entire twenty minutes she'd spent in Rose's apartment had had a surreal quality. She couldn't quite seem to grasp that this was really happening, as if the whole scene might be just another daydream.

Rose reached to dial Tom's number, then stopped, hand in midair, and bit her lip. "Uh, Melissa...why don't you go home and check with your parents about the condo? I'll try Tom and let you know about tomorrow."

"Yeah. Okay. Great." Melissa gulped the last of her tea and beat a hasty retreat. Back in her apartment, she called her parents, hands shaking. What was she going to say? Hi, Mom, hi, Dad. I need to rent our condo to a friend in exchange for wild sex with a guy I don't know. Would that be okay?

Her dad answered and summoned her mom to the

phone. Somehow, Melissa managed to stammer out the request, brushing aside their numerous concerned questions. Yes, she was fine, just a little tired. Yes, the job was great. Yes, she was eating well. No, she didn't miss Bill. Okay, no problem, bye.

Poor Rose. Melissa hung up the phone, disappointed. Her parents were opening the condo early this year, to celebrate their fortieth anniversary over Fourth of July weekend.

Immediately a knock sounded on the door. It was Rose, looking a little anxious. "Did they say it was okay?"

"I'm sorry. They're using the place this weekend. They almost never go up this early. I didn't expect it to be a problem."

"Oh." Rose tried to smile, but it was a ghastly effort. "Thanks for trying."

Melissa looked at her curiously, wondering exactly what she was so eager to get away from. Maybe one of her guys had turned stalker on her. "Rose, are you—"

"I spoke to Tom." Rose broke in nervously, as if she knew what the question would be. "You're all set."

"Oh?" Melissa's voice yodeled on the one syllable. This was it. Another step along the way; another part of the transition into the woman she hoped to explore.

Help.

"Eight o'clock, tomorrow night. My place." Rose cracked a brittle smile, not quite meeting Melissa's eyes. "He said it'll be his pleasure."

"I HAVE A *DATE* TOMORROW?" Riley stopped, one foot-long sub sandwich in each hand, and curled his lip at his grinning friend. "I was going to take Leo to the movies so my sister could have an evening to herself."

"I know little Leo needs a man in his life, but so, apparently, does the fair Miss Rose. You get to be some guy named Tom." Slate leaned back in his chair and raised his eyebrows suggestively, obviously relishing being back in the trenches. "She wants sex lessons."

"*Sex lessons?* You have got to be kidding." Riley grabbed plates from his cabinet and plunked the sandwiches down, feeling as if he'd eaten something rotten. This Rose person was bad news. "Why the hell would a woman like that need lessons?"

Slate shrugged. "I guess even professionals like to keep in shape, though according to the Feds she's not actually a hooker."

"Just your friendly neighborhood hedonist. Not a hell of a lot of difference if you ask me." Riley banged the plates on the Shaker-style table he'd made in his basement workshop, his stomach churning. *Sex lessons.* Of all the stupid games…with something that should be so natural. "Are you sure you heard right? It wasn't Tom that needed the lessons from her?"

"I'm sure. I'm guessing playing teacher floats Tommy's salami." Slate took a huge bite of his sub and chewed; his boyish blue eyes crinkled mischievously. "Some guys are into that stuff."

"Oh, *man.*" Riley took a swig of milk and pushed his plate away. "They didn't train me for this in the marines."

"You'd rather penetrate Iraqi lines than the fair Ms. Rose?"

Riley glared at him. "Forget lessons. I'll show up as the plumber."

"And investigate her pipes?" Slate blinked innocently as Riley rolled his eyes in disgust. "This is the perfect setup, Riley. If you can't find the portrait the good senator ditched with her on the first go-around, you have a good excuse to go back—provided you can find something to teach her."

Riley dropped his head in his hands and groaned. He'd have to call Karen and reschedule the time with Leo. Slate was making too much sense. The FBI had backed Captain Watson's insistence that Riley develop a friendship with Rose so he could search the apartment and find out what she knew.

Unfortunately, any searching while she was gone would attract undesired attention to the Feds' involvement in the case. Her place was being watched by the cops *and* Jake Allston, the crime boss who'd originally bribed Senator Mason with the portrait, and who wanted to keep it out of the hands of the police so it wouldn't become crucial evidence in a trial against him.

Riley raised his head and sighed wearily. "Rose doesn't know this guy?"

"Nope. They've never met. But her reputation must have preceded her. The guy was drooling all over the phone. You should have heard her work him. Man! She was something." Slate put his sandwich down and crossed his arms over his chest, hands in his armpits—his characteristic gesture when something unsettled him. "Funny thing, though, I got the feeling that underneath, she's scared to death. I'm betting Miss Rose is in this way over her head."

Something in Slate's voice snapped Riley out of

his self-pity. He stared at his friend. "Oh? Why don't *you* take this one, Slate? You've been in Maine for a long time. You must have gotten pretty lonely."

Slate held up his hands in surrender. "Not me. You're the one Captain Watson asked to do the job. The Feds want the police kept happy while they check out who's leaking information to Allston's men. Besides, you're the international sexpert around here, if our time overseas was anything to go by." He made a face and jerked his thumb to his chest. "I was the sucker with the girl back home."

Riley nodded, shoving back the sympathy he knew his friend hated. Slate had been faithful in the face of endless temptation. Unfortunately, his girlfriend hadn't seen fit to return the favor. Not surprisingly, Slate had taken it hard. His mother's death over the past long year hadn't helped. When he'd showed up on Riley's doorstep the day before, thin and down, Riley had been shocked. Today was the first sign of the return of his humor and sense of fun—the perfect cover for the brilliant, ruthless operator he was. Riley had done well inviting him to be in on this case. The FBI wasn't known for granting favors, but they'd let Slate in with a surprising lack of protest. Apparently Gemini's reputation extended beyond the military.

"And I've got a hot date, too, with the real Tom." Slate grinned around a mouthful of cold cuts. "To make sure he has lots and lots of other plans until this operation is over."

"And then?"

"Then I get to kick back and be available. I might be useful, since I'm invisible as far as the cops are concerned."

"And as far as Jake Allston's people are concerned." Riley resignedly pulled his plate closer and started on his sandwich. Unfortunately, he had to admit he *was* the right man for the job. The stolen miniature of Queen Elizabeth was the crucial link needed to prove Senator Mason's involvement in Jake Allston's corrupt empire. Allston had used it to bribe the art-loving senator in return for legislation favoring Allston's business interests. With the portrait, the Feds could grant Mason immunity from prosecution in exchange for his testimony against Allston. Since Riley had been invited in by the police, his involvement would create a buffer zone between the Feds and the cops while the Feds investigated the leak in the force. All the pieces fit. Everyone was happy.

Except Riley.

He felt as if he'd been assigned to seduce a viper. Not that Rose would need much seducing, unless she and Tom did have some master-slave thing to act out. In that case, he'd have to pretend to seduce her, while they both knew the entire scene was a bunch of crap. He swallowed a bite; the bread tasted like glue in his dry mouth.

Sex between a man and a woman was supposed to flow, to evolve naturally out of mutual desires and tastes. It wasn't something you should have to program or teach. Experimenting was all very well; he'd done his share. But how much better to lie together and simply savor what all humans were born to do.

He washed down the glue with a swallow of milk. He'd have to try damn hard either to find the portrait right away, since Captain Watson and the Feds seemed so certain it was in Rose's apartment, or be absolutely, one-hundred-percent sure it was somewhere else.

ROSE CRAMMED FIVE PAIRS of underwear, two bras, three T-shirts, two pairs of shorts, two mini-sundresses, deodorant, shampoo and a toothbrush into the largest purse she owned, her movements jerky and hurried. She wasn't sure where she was going yet. Once she got to South Station she could decide. Her budget would only allow travel by train, but she couldn't pass up this opportunity to leave.

Melissa would be in her apartment in an hour; anyone keeping an eye on the place would see a slender young woman entertaining a man. Nothing so unusual about that. Rose had been careful on the phone, with Melissa out of the room, to make it seem as if Tom would be meeting *her* tonight, in case her phone was being tapped. He'd sounded so eager and had accepted the "teacher" role so readily, she felt horrible leaving Melissa to face him. But they'd work it out. Or not. Either way, by the time whoever wanted her—or whatever he thought she had—found out she was missing, Rose would be long gone.

If things didn't work out with Tom, Melissa would go back to her own apartment and her own life, and only wonder once in a while where her neighbor had gone. If things *did* work out, no doubt she and Tom would use Melissa's own apartment after tonight. Melissa would be in no danger—of that Rose felt sure, or she wouldn't be doing this.

She'd considered slipping a note under Melissa's door, explaining the switch, but after seeing the horror of nerves on Melissa's face when Rose announced that the date had been set, she knew her neighbor wouldn't show if she thought Tom expected Rose herself. And Rose really needed Melissa to be in the apartment tonight. Just tonight. So she'd have a chance to escape.

She slung the bulging bag over her shoulder, hoping it wouldn't be obvious that it contained more than the usual purse items. After one last look in the mirror to adjust her blond wig, check her makeup, fasten a sweater over her bare shoulders and flowered sundress, Rose let herself out of the apartment and slid her key under Melissa's door as planned. Too impatient to wait for the elevator, she took the stairs down three floors to the basement and slipped out the back entrance.

On the way to the Harvard Square T stop, and on the ride from Cambridge to Boston, she channeled her nervous energy into looking happy and carefree—a woman out on a shopping spree, planning to return home tonight for a romantic assignation with Tall Dark and Handsome. She got off at South Station, checking as casually as she could for anyone else leaving the train who might seem unduly interested in her and where she was going.

Then she hurried up the escalator and lunged toward the turnstile, at the exact same moment as a distinctly male body wearing a T-shirt and jeans.

"Sorry. After you." The distinctly male body stepped back and gestured her through. She turned, looked up and met a pair of dynamite blue eyes under short, military-style blond hair. Eyes brimming with boyish humor, intelligence, warmth and a touch of something grim and steely that even in Rose's near-frantic state fascinated her.

She smiled her thanks and pushed through the turnstile ahead of him, wishing it was some other day and that she was, in fact, on the mindless, infinitely cancelable errand she wanted everyone to think she was on. Then she could take time to delve into those eyes and what lay behind them. It had been awhile since she'd gotten to know someone close to her age.

"I'm Mike. Slater. Friends call me Slate. What's your name?" He fell into step beside her, fanning the spark of her regret into a painful ember.

"I'm Rose. Just Rose. Friends call me Rose." She sent him an I'm-only-teasing smile so he wouldn't think she was making fun of him. Guys hated being made fun of. Their egos couldn't stand it. Though this one seemed so natural and boy-next-door in spite of his incredible sex appeal, he might not have minded.

"Where you headed?"

"Train station." Her smile grew wary. Even a natural, heavenly built boy-next-door could be a threat. Someone out to make sure she disappeared, one way or the other. Or someone trying to keep her from leaving.

Rose clenched her teeth. She hated this. Hated not being able to trust anyone. Hated that everything and everyone might be something other than they seemed. That this nice-looking guy might be about to drag her out to some deserted lot and threaten to shoot her for whatever he thought she'd done, or whatever he thought she had.

The sooner she was out of Boston, the better. Even by talking to this guy, even if he was innocent, she'd already attracted someone's attention. Someone who could answer questions about her if he bumped into people who wanted to know. As much as she wanted to linger and listen and look, she had to get rid of him.

"What time's your train?"

"I'm not…it's not for a while." Only a few dozen yards into the crowded main room of the station she'd be able to see the departure schedule and take her pick of time and destination. Why couldn't he have waited to ask until then, so it wouldn't be so obvious she had no idea where she was going?

"I've got a long wait, too. I'm meeting a friend. Can I buy you a drink?"

"Oh, gosh. I don't think so, thanks." She quickened her pace; he kept up easily.

"I just want to buy you a drink, that's it. Juice, milk, soda, whatever…doesn't have to be booze."

"No, really. I'm fine."

"I don't mind. There are some decent places here." He gestured toward the assortment of eateries in the station.

Rose stopped and turned to face him, struck again by the depth and complexity of the expression in his eyes. "Are you always this persistent?"

"No." He grinned and crossed his arms, hands shoved into his armpits. "Usually I don't even ask in the first place. So I guess I don't want to start off a career of asking strange women out with a dismal failure."

She couldn't help a small smile. This guy would probably be a lot of fun. Damn the timing all to hell.

"I'm sorry. I just have to be so careful." She bit her lip. "Everyone has to be careful these days."

"Okay, no problem." He held up his hands and backed away. "Nice to meet you, Rose. Have a good trip."

He grinned once more and strode off toward the food court. She took a quick, deep breath. Stupid as it sounded, and as much as she had been anxious to shake him off, now that he was gone, she felt terribly alone.

She pulled herself together, scanned the departure board, chose a train to D.C., so she'd have the most stops to choose from, bought her ticket and a newspaper, and settled down to wait.

3

MELISSA SAT ON HER discarded-outfit littered bed,
hands tucked under her thighs, knees pressed together, feet pressed together. She had a good view in
the dresser mirror opposite her, so she could see first-
hand what she looked like when she was panicking.

Not a pretty sight. Her eyes were huge, her face so
pale that the makeup she'd put on looked like it was
trying to bring her back from the dead. Her jaw was
so tight her teeth were starting to ache, and when she
brought her hand up to tuck her hair behind her ears,
forgetting her hair wasn't long enough to tuck anymore, her hand was shaking. In fact, her entire body
was shaking.

She glanced at the clock. Seven-fifty. In ten
minutes she'd go across the hall and do some shaking
there. Seeing as guys were always late, at eight-fifteen
this Tom person would waltz in. He'd be overly handsome, with tufts of chest hair that poked all the way
up to his Adam's apple. He'd have several gold neck-
laces glinting through the unbuttoned opening of his
rayon shirt, and he'd make that horrible gun with his
fingers and pretend to shoot her in greeting. Which
was a damn strange way to be charming, now that
she thought about it.

No way. She couldn't do this. She was not a sex
goddess. She belonged with someone dependable and

a little dull, someone like Bill. She should be married, cheerfully and gracefully pregnant, glowing with peace and good health, helping her husband make their bed in the morning.

She shuddered. Ick. Not yet. Not until she was thirty, anyway. She needed this time to explore, this last chance in her life to check out the wild side. Each of her relationships had lasted longer than the previous one, and she had a feeling Mr. Right would show up soon. So what was wrong with something before then? A little stopgap? Better to screw around now than do it after she was married. Or wonder the rest of her life what a fling would feel like. Right?

Right.

She glanced at the clock again. A little sideways flirt of a glance, so that maybe if she took only the tiniest look, time would slow down a little, or maybe stop, and she wouldn't ever have to go in there and meet him.

Tom would hook his jacket over one finger on his shoulder and wink at her as if she was a cute child. He'd be too huge and musclebound, the kind of guy who'd have to turn sideways to fit through the door, and who'd have no spit at all and kiss her with a dry mouth that he used special lip weights to keep young and firm. The kind of guy who called women he was trying to impress "kid" or "babe."

Ick.

No way. She couldn't do this. What were the odds that he would be attractive to her? How many men did she pass in the street, and how many of them *were*? Really attractive? Enough to want to touch? Hardly any.

So Rose thought he was sexy. Rose dated men old

enough to be her father, who had paunches and horrible taste in clothes and probably bad breath and erectile dysfunction.

What the hell am I doing?

The traitorous clock now said 7:58. Melissa took a shaky breath and moved her shaky body over to the dresser. She picked up the key with her shaky hand, her shaky brain still not sure if she was actually going to use the key. But she had to. She couldn't stand him up. She couldn't bear the curiosity for the rest of her life if she never even got a peek at him. And she wasn't going to stoop to peering through the doorway and only coming out if he was cute.

For one thing, she didn't want him to know she even lived in this building until she decided whether he was someone she'd like to…get to know.

She opened her door and raced across to Rose's apartment, managed to fit the key into the lock and went inside, trying to take deep breaths into lungs that had developed some kind of weird stuttering problem. She would have loved a small drink—say, a fifth or so of Scotch—but she didn't drink that much, and wouldn't want him to smell it on her if he got close enough to.

Oh, God. What was she doing? What if he was totally wonderful? How could she stop herself from falling in love with him? What made her think she was emotionally equipped for intimacy without feeling?

She went over to the window and opened it, thankful for the cool night air that flowed into Rose's apartment. If it was humid and oppressive, she'd probably pass out. She looked down into the street, hoping to catch a glimpse of the guy so she could at least get a preview.

No studs. All she saw was that parked TV repair truck, which must belong to someone who had recently moved onto their street.

The knock on the door was perfect. Not loud and insistent. Not timid. Not silly and overly rhythmic. Confident, firm-knuckled, let me in.

Oh, help. Let him in.

She took a huge deep breath, which her lungs suddenly allowed her to have, and went to open the door.

He was perfect.

He was so perfect she wanted to laugh. He was so perfect she wanted to cry. He was so perfect she just stood there and stared and thought about how perfect he was until it occurred to her she was being totally ridiculous.

"Hi, Tom. Come in."

He nodded. Even his nod was perfect. Up and down of his head, with his firm jaw starting it and his high forehead following. Dark, dark hair, slightly wavy and thick, dynamite brown eyes surprisingly light in color, long lashes, nice mouth, a sexy groove running down one cheek.

She moved back into Rose's overdecorated apartment and gestured him in, then closed the door and watched as he walked into the room and looked around.

Perfect. Tall, not too tall; built, not too built. Jacket and tie, respectable, well-groomed. Perfect.

And the most perfect thing of all was that he was *so* perfect, there wasn't the slightest chance she'd fall in love with him. Who the hell wanted to stare at someone that perfect for the rest of her life? Talk about feeling inadequate.

He swung around and met her gaze, a faint smile deepening that groove in his right cheek. His eyes were penetrating, his expression slightly cynical, totally exciting. She found herself beaming back in breathless, idiotic, hopeful happiness. This could actually work.

"Call me Riley." His voice was perfect, too, of course. Deep and rich, the kind of voice that went through you and curled your toes. "It's my middle name. Only my mom and Amanda call me Tom."

"Riley." She nodded and stood there. He stood there, too, and she started feeling a little uneasy. He didn't seem the type for polite small talk. And now that she thought about it, his stare was making her uncomfortable. There was something sort of speculative in it, something almost…disdainful.

Then it hit her. He didn't find her attractive.

In a scene out of an alchemist's nightmare, the gold excitement in her chest turned to lead misery and sank into her stomach. Of course. Mr. Perfect would want Ms. Perfect. Rose probably had told him she was Demi Moore's double to get him to come.

"Do you want a drink, Riley?" Because she sure as hell did. "Scotch okay?"

He nodded. She moved to the tray she'd brought in earlier from her place, and poured out two stiff drinks. While she did this, Tom-now-Riley walked around the apartment, examining Rose's clutter of knickknacks: her collection of still-life paintings, sometimes two deep on the red walls; the bowls of potpourri that made the room smell like some anonymous chemist's idea of fresh.

Melissa crossed to him and handed him his drink. "Cheers."

She raised her glass in salute, then drained half of it.

He lifted an eyebrow. "Thirsty?"

She smiled and laughed somewhat stupidly, which was very un-perfect of her. "Nervous."

He nodded, which seemed to be his preferred mode of communication. That weird judgmental expression was still on his face. In spite of the fact that he was perfect, and mysterious, and sort of terrifying in a dangerous, wildly erotic way, she was also starting to find him a little annoying. If he thought what she wanted was so disgusting, why had he come? If he thought she was so disgusting, why didn't he leave? He didn't seem the type to worry about politeness.

"So." She folded her arms across her chest and exhaled a short, forced breath. *To hell with him.* "How about those Red Sox?"

His grin was slow and surprising, spreading across his face and making grooves in both cheeks, a double in the right one. She couldn't help smiling back. You couldn't be in the room with a man who smiled at you that way and not smile back. Even if you sort of wanted to slug him in the gut.

"Think they'll go all the way this year?" She opened her eyes wide and blinked repeatedly.

He actually chuckled that time. Then he took a healthy swallow of Scotch and put it down behind him on Rose's mantel, without looking, as if he simply sensed it was there. He stood, hands on his hips pushing back his jacket, staring at her with an intimate I-know-what-we're-going-to-be-doing-later look in his eyes.

Melissa drew in her breath. Her face turned cold and probably pale, then reheated in a flush of warmth that spread down her body and made her skin feel as if it was reaching out to be touched. *Oh. My. Lord.* The man could seduce a nun. Maybe he did find her the tiniest bit attractive, after all. Or maybe he'd promised Rose and felt he had to.

Whatever. Melissa wasn't ready to get cozy yet, not until she'd figured out his strange attitude. And she had this thing about not kissing men until they'd uttered at least four complete sentences.

She backed away and gestured toward the couch with her drink, nearly spilling it in the process. "Would you like to sit down?"

He sat in the burgundy wing chair, the lace antimacassar looking idiotically feminine and out of place behind him.

Melissa gulped more of her drink, its tingly warmth adding to what she already felt from Mr. Perfect's incredible sex appeal. Maybe if he'd actually *talk* she wouldn't be so freaked out.

"Why are you nervous?"

She barely escaped choking on her Scotch. What the hell did he think? If she hadn't seen the piercing intelligence in those eyes, she'd wonder about his brain power. "I don't exactly do this often."

"No."

She snapped her head up and gaped at him. He kept his gaze level, unperturbed, slightly challenging. Something in the way he'd said "no" did what women had been fighting against for generations: it meant yes. It meant he thought she invited strange men over to explore her sexuality all the time.

"Excuse me?" She stood up, feeling slightly unsteady, beginning to be annoyed in earnest. "Would you mind lifting yourself above the four-word sentence and explaining that?"

He leaned back in his chair. "Do I need to?"

She came very, very close to flinging her drink in his lap. Instead she slammed it down on Rose's brass table. What a total jerk. This was a major disaster. And he'd been so—

She wasn't going to use that *p* word again. Not for a jerk, not even a perfect jerk.

She pointed furiously down at her shoes. "Flats, so you wouldn't think I'm a tramp, and because I was worried you might not be tall. Knee skirt, plain navy, no sit-down wrinkles across the front—i.e., not too short, not too tight. Basic off-white top, normal makeup, plain old hair. All calculated during the last nearly sleepless twenty-four hours in an obsessive and carefully laid plan, to ensure that if you didn't find me attractive, or if I didn't find *you* attractive, the rejection would be minimal because I didn't go all out for seduction."

She jerked her arm straight out in front of her. "Observe the shaking hand, complete with sweaty palm. If you'd like to feel my pulse I think you'll find it one step shy of panic level. Now. Please tell me exactly *what* would make you think I've done this before."

His eyes narrowed, then his expression changed to contain something that seemed like admiration. He grinned that slow sexy grin which changed him from terrifying to devastating. "I apologize. You're perfect."

Melissa would have laughed, except he sounded like he was mocking her, and she was still furious.

He thought *she* was perfect? "Two sentences that time. I dare you to up the count."

He stood and took a step toward her. "I'm not much of a talker."

The implication was there, in his eyes, in his purposeful nearness. *I'm better at other things.* Melissa reached down for her drink and walked toward Rose's tiny kitchenette, unsettled to the verge of tears. She wasn't ready. She wasn't sure she'd ever be ready for this man. Two minutes into their meeting he was playing mind games, and she hadn't a clue why. Maybe he thought it was sexy. Maybe he thought making his victims want to stick pins in him would be fabulous foreplay.

It wasn't. Not even close.

She drained her glass and poured herself another Scotch, knowing she wouldn't be able to come close to drinking even half of it. She'd rather not exhaust her dignity by throwing up in Rose's toilet. But it gave her something to do, something to help her escape his calculating stares and overwhelming presence. Something to help calm her while she figured out how to get the evening back on track.

"Look, Riley." She clenched the whiskey bottle, not yet brave enough to turn around and face him. "I'm kind of a mess over this whole thing. So if you could make it a little easier on me, I'd appreciate it. I don't know what you expected, but obviously I'm not it."

She took a long, healing breath, glad to have all that out in the open…and held it. He'd come up behind her. Close. She could feel his warmth, could feel his eyes on her. She wished her hair was still long so the back of her neck wouldn't feel so exposed. Her sleeveless cotton shirt had only a slightly scooped front and back, but she might as well have been wearing a bikini top, the way she felt.

"You're better than I expected." He drew his hands down her arms in a light, caressing touch that ended with him circling her wrists in a firm grip she had a feeling would tighten impossibly if she tried to pull away. Although his tone still hovered between compliment and insult, Melissa's heartbeat sped up. She stood entranced, imprisoned, and somewhat shamefully aroused.

"I expected you'd be beautiful." He said the words softly into the top of her hair. She felt as if his voice was surrounding her, heating her, making her joints go watery.

Beautiful? No way. "Pretty"—she'd been called that. "Cute" tons of times—she hated that. Beautiful?

"I expected you'd be desirable." He drew his hands back up to her shoulders and let go lingeringly. "But I didn't expect such…perfect innocence, for all I was warned. You're quite a woman."

Melissa swallowed. Warned? Rose thought Melissa was so virginal she had to *warn* him? "Uh, thank you? I'm not really sure what you…I mean, I'm not *that* innocent, but I am… I mean, it *is* kind of the whole point of you being here, isn't it?"

"Yes." He laughed without humor. "Of course."

Melissa sidled away, putting distance between herself and this totally confusing person. She felt off balance and infuriated, and infatuated, and inebriated and pretty much anything else anyone cared to mention. This had to have been the most confusing half hour of her life. But one thing had been totally decided the minute he touched her, the minute he half whispered words into her hair. She wanted him. As soon as they got past this strange tension, she wanted him to be the one. Rose's instincts were absolutely right on. This was a man she could stock ice cubes and honey for. But how the hell to get to that point?

Maybe if she got him away from the mind games, maybe if they got to the, uh, purpose of the evening, they could put this bizarre uncomfortable beginning behind them. She took a deep breath and crossed her fingers.

"So. How do you usually…I mean, do you want to talk first or just… Oh, forget it. I stink at this." She put her drink down and turned in exasperation. "Can we just—"

He was right there. Somehow he'd moved while she'd been thinking and stuttering, and he was right there. She froze, whatever asinine thing she'd been about to say still dangling from the end of her tongue.

He moved forward so his body was all of a half-inch from hers, smiling down with that strange, challenging, know-it-all smile that made her want to slug him and kiss him at the same time. He dipped his head slightly toward her, still holding her eyes with his penetrating brown gaze. "You first."

Melissa's eyes widened. "What?"

His smile stretched briefly. "I said, you first."

"But…*you're* supposed to—" Melissa closed her eyes. Okay. So he wasn't going to take the lead. She could kiss him. She'd done that before. She could do this. To hell with him.

She opened her eyes to find him still there, still staring, still with that smug, annoying-as-hell smirk. Her anger rose. Fine. *Jackass.* She lifted on tiptoes and planted a loud, closemouthed, little girl smack on

his lips, complete with sound effects. "Mmm-ah."
Then she went back down on her heels, shrugged and
batted her eyes with rhythmic fluttery precision.
"Well, gee. That's about the best I can do. You really
have your work cut out for you, Riley."

For a second she wasn't sure what he would do,
and it suddenly occurred to her that if he got angry,
she could be a squashed bug under his fist in about
ten seconds. She'd never felt physically vulnerable
around a man, and it scared her.

If the sick truth be told, it fascinated her, too. And
aroused her. She suddenly pictured him picking her
up and taking her right here, standing in the middle
of the room with her legs hooked around him, while
he held her up with nothing but the strength in his
shoulders.

All of which would not come to pass if he killed
her now.

He didn't. He pulled her against him and kissed her
long and hard, a mean, messy kiss that left her feeling
punished and violated and wanting to cry. "Is that
what you wanted me to teach you?"

"No." She turned away; he followed, grabbed her
arms, lifted her up onto the kitchen table and pushed
himself between her legs.

"How about this?"

"What are you *doing?*" She could barely gasp the
words out. This was beyond horrible. Her worst nightmare. The man was a brutal, sick, macho pig and he
was going to rape her, and it was partly her fault for
coming up with this stupid idea in the first place. She
pushed at his shoulders ineffectually, knowing she
was totally powerless to keep him from doing anything he wanted. "Stop it. *Stop!*"

He drew back and looked at her incredulously. She didn't move, other than to make strange uncontrollable sobbing noises without tears, breath heaving to get out of her chest.

"What the—" He narrowed his eyes and swore obscenely. "I can't figure you out at all."

"What do you *mean?* I'm the most straightforward person on the planet." Tears spilled out of her eyes and onto her cheeks. "You're the weird one. You come in here and start playing bizarre mind games. It's like you hated me from the beginning. If you don't want to be here why the hell did you come?"

He stared at her again, as if he didn't speak her language and had no clue what she'd been trying to tell him. Then he released her and walked away, stood by the window, a big, male, solitary figure against the white lace curtains blowing in the soft evening air.

Melissa got down from the table, shaken and crying, and reached for a tissue from the lacquered box on Rose's counter.

"How many men have you had sex with?"

She started. "What?"

He repeated the question, searching her face from across the room as if he thought her answer was the key to something mystical and life-saving.

She sank into an antique rocking chair and blew her nose loudly, not caring if she looked like Rudolph the Red-nosed Reindeer when she'd finished. Not caring about anything except the immense relief that he'd morphed back into the harmless sexy man he'd been when he first came in. Somehow, even in her badly shaken state, it was slowly entering her awareness that something—maybe something he'd misunderstood from his buddy Rose—had made him think badly of her. And even if it made her a spineless wimp, she desperately wanted to change his mind, to make it right, so they could start again with something approaching a normal meeting, and see if they could work things out.

"Only two. Two men. One in college—it hurt and it was horrible. Then Bill—it didn't hurt, but it was still pretty horrible."

"No others?"

She tossed her tissues into a wicker wastebasket, so drained and stripped emotionally that baring her sex life to a stranger seemed the most natural thing in the world. "The others were just dates. Just fun."

He nodded, looked at her intently, as if he was making up his mind about something. Melissa could even sense the minute he changed his attitude, when his eyes and mouth softened into something strangely guilty and almost tender, and she wanted to cry again, from relief this time.

He crossed the room and crouched in front of her, his huge body compacting lightly and effortlessly. He put his hands on the outside of her thighs and looked up at her, his expression open and sincere for the first time since he'd come in.

"Tell me what you want from me, Rose."

She almost laughed at his slip, except that she wasn't capable of laughter at that moment. "It's Melissa."

He didn't look remotely embarrassed by his mistake. "Melissa is your real name?"

"*Yes.*" She nearly cried again. Why couldn't he take anything at face value?

"Okay." He continued watching her closely. Very

closely, as if she were his science experiment. "What do you want from me, Melissa?"

She took a deep breath, trying to gather her emotions into some semblance of order. "I...I want to try new things. I want to be safe, but I want an adventure. Something I can remember when I'm fifty and have been under the same guy for twenty years. Anything...except pain or humiliation. Everything but the same old missionary grind."

"I understand." His hands slid up her thighs to her waist; he tightened his hold into a strong, reassuring grip, brown eyes holding hers intently. "I make it a habit always to trust my instincts over my information. For some reason, tonight I didn't. I made a mistake. I'm sorry."

Melissa gaped, certain he didn't make apologizing an everyday habit, and somewhat awed that he'd done it for her. "You thought I was a phony."

He grimaced. "Something like that."

"But *why?*" She practically shouted the word. What on earth had Rose told him?

"I thought you were playing a role. That this was all a game."

"I'm not, Riley. It's not a game, I promise." One more tear escaped and trickled down her cheek. He watched until it slid into the corner of her mouth, then stood, lifting her to her feet, and kissed her. Only this was nothing like the kissing he'd done before. Nothing mean or messy or punishing. This kiss was sweet, gentle, languorous, tasting the tear that had fallen on her lips, taking his time getting to know the shape of her mouth, each corner; each lip tugged, tasted, explored.

She pressed herself against him, shocked to feel

him hard between them. *Oh, man. He wanted her. A guy like this.* She could scarcely take it in. He wanted her.

He led her over to the couch, sat and pulled her down across his lap, still kissing her as if he didn't intend to stop for the rest of the evening. She sank against him, totally carried away by the man and his mouth, and managed only a slight moan of protest when he kissed a line from her lips to her throat and back along her jaw to behind her ear. His hands came up under her skirt, over her thighs, skimmed and settled on the mound of her sex through her panties.

Arousal seared through her; she gasped and arched up instinctively for more pressure, shocked by his boldness, shocked by her own. The nerves of the last few hours, the raw fear and subsequent safety, had fueled her; she'd never been this hot, this ready in such a short time. With his warm hand against her, she was burning nearly out of control, panting like an animal. If he touched her, she'd die. If he didn't, she'd die faster.

He pushed his hand under her panties, incredibly warm, incredibly strong, incredibly sure. She opened her legs shamelessly and shut her eyes, aware he was watching her face, but not wanting to be aware of anything except the need his touch aroused in her body. He found her wetness, slid his finger inside, then started a light regular stroking in and out, rubbing her gently with his thumb, stopping now and then to tease and dip inside her again.

Melissa lost herself. She was gone. Nowhere. Nothing existed except the unfamiliar fingers of this man's hand on and inside her, and the sensations he was making her feel. She squirmed against the coming climax, put it off, clenched her thighs to make him slow down. She wanted to feel like this forever.

He resisted, urged her on, pushed inside with two fingers, rubbed harder until she fell apart, gave in, let the burning current wash over her, let her muscles contract helplessly around his fingers, then subside.

She opened her eyes to find him still watching her, an incredulous expression on his face, the measuring look back in his eyes.

Melissa slid off his lap and fell onto the sofa beside him, dazed and flushed with passion, suddenly aware of how crazed she'd become, and embarrassed by it. How the hell could she let a stranger bring her so completely out of herself? Nothing even approaching that had ever happened to her.

She drew her hands down her face and throat and smiled at him shyly. "That was…nice." The word came out as the ridiculous understatement it was, which made him smile wryly. She glanced at his erection, which was making his lap a thing of beauty and astonishing magnitude. "Uh, can I…I mean, shouldn't I…do something for you?"

"No, thanks." He got up and adjusted himself under his pants. "I put you through a rough start tonight. I deserve to suffer."

"I don't mind, really. I can—"

"It's okay." He pulled her to her feet, brushed aside her bangs and released her. "I ought to get going."

"Oh." Melissa wrapped her arms around herself, shocked at his abrupt departure, then chided herself the next second. What did she expect? Affectionate nuzzling for three hours? "Okay."

He paused at the door, one hand on the knob on his way out. "When would you like to meet again?"

"Uh..." Her mind raced. *Would now be too soon?* Would he think she was too desperate if she suggested tomorrow or the next day? How long could she stand waiting for another adventure with him?

"Same time tomorrow?"

Yes! "That sounds..." She cringed. "I can't tomorrow. I have to work. Day after is fine, though."

She cleared her husky throat, trying to act as normal as possible scheduling sex with someone she'd just been intimate with and didn't know at all, when her insides were singing the "Star Spangled Banner" because he wanted to see her again so soon.

"Okay." He smiled under intense, serious eyes. "Day after tomorrow. See you then."

Melissa waved and closed the door, then turned and leaned back against it, eyes closed, mouth curved in a sappy, happy grin.

On impulse, she rushed to the window and watched until she saw him come out of the building and walk down Garden Street, confident, graceful, masculine. Until he went around the corner and disappeared.

Melissa straightened and slowly closed the window. Rose's unfamiliar, ultrafeminine apartment felt suddenly still and close and empty behind her.

Okay, Melissa. You asked for this and you got it. No strings. Just the physical. Just what you said you wanted.

She wrapped her arms around herself, lonely and bereft and unsatisfied in spite of the most amazing orgasm she'd ever experienced. What was the matter with her? She should be springing off the walls with self-satisfied happiness. She'd passed the test. She was desirable. He'd passed the test: he was so desirable as to redefine desirable. She'd have her fling, learn everything she could, explore her wild side and build up that stockpile of sensual memories she could draw on when Mr. Right and she were bored to death of each other.

Instead, she was standing here, wistfully staring out the window of an apartment that wasn't hers, wishing the man she prized for being totally uninvolved would come back to her and make her feel it all again.

4

"NOW BOARR-DING on Track number ten, the 8:10 Middleboro-Lakeville local." The deep, amplified voice echoed through the station. Diesel fumes wafted through the doors to the tracks, punctuating the announcement. Rose closed her newspaper, stretched her legs impatiently and glanced at her watch for the millionth time. Eight o'clock. Her train wasn't due for another forty-five minutes.

According to her calculations, several years had gone by since she'd arrived at the station, but her watch insisted it had been only a little under an hour. She folded the paper and slapped it down on the wrought-iron table in front of her. To hell with sitting. Her brain would explode if she had to try and force herself to read for another second.

She got up and walked over to the newsstand in the center of the station. Maybe a celebrity magazine—some gossipy rag to distract her until she could get on the train and go somewhere to feel safe again. Her plan was simple. She'd choose a stop on the way to D.C. and wait until the last possible second to get off the train, to avoid being followed. Then she'd wait for whatever next train pulled in, and repeat the process until she was sure no one had any idea where she was.

From there she'd see about finding somewhere inexpensive to stay. Maybe she could even find a man in need of company for a while. She had two weeks vacation from her secretary job at Harvard. Her boss had griped briefly about her impulsive decision to take time off, but had grudgingly agreed when she turned on the charm.

In two weeks she'd call Senator Sleazeball and find out how things stood. She wasn't ready to leave Boston permanently. There had to be some way to clear—

"Well, if it isn't our good friend Rose."

The unfamiliar nasal voice behind her made her stomach contract in fear. She swung around and found herself staring up at two enormous men in suits and ties, both smiling too politely.

She swallowed and attempted an answering smile, heart hammering in her chest. For God's sake, the men were goons sent to stop her from leaving. Exactly what she'd feared, but deep down she hadn't really believed possible. The whole idea was so ludicrously overdramatic. One man even had a crooked nose, broken too many times, with a scar across the tip; the other had gelled-back raven hair and connecting eyebrows.

"I'm sorry—" she glanced between them, fighting down the adrenaline pouring through her body "—do I know you?"

Broken Nose bowed slightly. "Let's just say we have mutual acquaintances."

"I see." Rose clutched her bag, trying desperately to appear unworried, feeling as if she'd been thrust into some cheesy gangster movie. Her senses were on overdrive, eyes seeing everything too brightly, a peculiar rushing noise in her ears. Details stuck out in startling clarity—the tiny blue thread on Broken

Nose's lapel; the shining clumps of Gel Man's thick hair, combed back into rigid furrows.

Half of her wanted to run screaming out of the station, and the other half wanted to speed up the surreal, slow-motion passage of time, speak reasonably to the men and ask them if they had any idea what stereotypes they were, and had they really wanted their lives to turn out like this?

Instead, she stayed where she was, carrying on the obvious charade of pretending she had no idea they were going to threaten her, bully her, and who knew what else.

"Well." Her voice came out unnaturally high and breathy. "I'm here to meet a friend."

"That's nice." Broken Nose beamed, apparently intensely happy for her. "But we need you to take a little walk with us first."

Rose opened her mouth and a strange gasping sound came out, almost like laughter, but laced with panic. This was ridiculous. This couldn't be happening. She glanced desperately toward the food court, where she'd last seen that Slate guy, and came up empty. Where the hell was Sir Galahad when you needed him most? Not that she'd want to put anyone in danger on her account. But an ally would be pretty damn wonderful right about now.

She lifted her chin and glared. "What do you want from me?"

"Just a nice walk and a little chat. That's all." Gel Man stepped closer, still smiling politely, and reached for her arm.

"Don't touch me." The response was automatic. She backed away from his grasp, all pretense at composure gone. "I'll scream if you touch me."

"Now, Rose." Gel Man's smile grew wider. "Let's not—"

"Rose! I can't *believe* it! It's *Rose!*" Strong hands locked onto her waist and turned her away from her worst nightmare toward the fabulously familiar, mom-'n-apple-pie grinning face of Sir My-friends-call-me-Slate Galahad. "Gosh, Rose! How long has it been? Five years? You look fabulous."

He drew her into a hearty, gee-whiz embrace with a solid core of safety and reassurance.

"You…look great, too." She barely managed to croak out the words, weak with the bizarre swirling of relief and lingering fear. "Wonderful, in fact."

"Five years." He gave an awestruck whistle. "So, what are you up these days?"

"I'm…living here, working…." She gazed at him stupidly, clinging to the sight as if she could blot out the existence of the other men by concentrating hard enough on his boyish strength. Would they leave her alone now? Would they wait? Would they see through Slate's rescue attempt and get him in trouble, too?

"I live in Framingham these days." He put his hand over his heart and beamed proudly. "I'm a cop. A lieutenant. Just like I always said I would be."

"A Lieutenant!" She gave a near-hysterical giggle. "I am *so* happy to hear that."

"Hey! Are these guys your friends?" He grinned at the two suddenly uncomfortable-looking men and hauled Rose against his side. "Sorry to hog this little gal to myself. I'm just so damn glad to see her after all this time. Always was crazy about her."

"Uh, no problem. We were just leaving." Broken Nose backed away a few steps.

"Have a nice reunion." Gel Man took a few more

steps back, pinning Rose with a warm smile that left her icy. "We'll see you later, Rose."

They turned and hurried back through the station toward the street, where they'd undoubtedly take up watch for her again. Rose shuddered, stepped reluctantly out of Slate's secure hold and smiled ruefully up at him.

"Thank you. For lack of anything remotely adequate to say...thank you."

He nodded, all the gosh-'n-by-golly gone from his manner, and stared at her from his over-six-foot height. "Are you in some kind of trouble?"

"I...apparently." Her body started to tremble. "Apparently, I am. Are you really a cop?"

"Nope. But they don't know that." He took her elbow and led her over to a nearby chair. "Sit and try to relax. If your body wants to shake, let it. I'll get you something to drink."

He strode over to Auntie Annie's Pretzel Stand, counted out exact change for a bottle of water, and strode back, the picture of take-charge efficiency. Rose accepted the water gratefully, his attitude even more gratefully, and gripped the bottle to keep it steady.

Slate lowered himself into the seat next to her and watched her drink. "Maybe I should have gotten you something stronger."

She shook her head. "This is fine. This is wonderful. Thank you."

He put one hand on the back of her chair, the other on the table in front of her, and leaned toward her, so that she felt further bolstered and embraced by his presence. "What did they want, Rose?"

"I don't know. That's the horror of it." She gestured helplessly. "I know it sounds ridiculous, but it's true. I must have done something, pissed someone off. I don't know, honestly."

His blue eyes narrowed slightly, considering her. She returned his gaze as earnestly as she could, willing him with everything in her soul to believe her. Right now, in the crowded bustle of the station, she felt as if this beautiful stranger who'd risked who-knew-what to help her was her only link to humanity.

"Have you been to the police?"

"Yes." She turned the half-empty water bottle around and around with hands that still shook. "They can't help me. Nothing's happened to me yet."

He nodded grimly, then leaned closer, eyes intent. "I know you have no reason to trust me, but I'd like to help you."

His voice was low, quiet, reassuring—a voice to gain the trust of a wounded animal. Rose shook her head, wanting to shout yes, please, anything, just get me out of this place in one piece.

"What about your friend?"

"His train is due soon. He's visiting a bunch of us—no problem if he stays with someone else."

"But I couldn't ask you to—"

"You're not asking. I'm offering." He touched her shoulder, a brief warm pressure. "Will you let me help you?"

His gentleness undid her. She shivered and blinked fiercely to beat back the tears.

"Thank you. Again, thank you. But only if you happen to know of a place in the absolute middle of nowhere where I can disappear for a couple of weeks."

His mouth spread slowly into a wide grin. He took

the bottle from her fingers and drew her to her feet. "Believe it or not, Rose, I know just the place."

RILEY EASED THE OAK BOARD up against the fence on his table saw and made a guided, controlled pass, slicing a cut exactly on his measure, precisely perpendicular. A satisfied smile curled his lips. *Yes.* Clean lines, square angles. Another perfect drawer front for the dresser he was making his nephew, Leo. Just what he needed to balance this strange mood.

"What the..."

He stared at the wood in his hands, unable to believe his carelessness. He'd cut the perfect drawer front from a piece already measured and cut for the side of the dresser. When was the last time he'd made a mistake that stupid? Not since he'd been a rank beginner, almost two decades ago. He should have known better than to try anything needing concentration when he was feeling so uncharacteristically... unsettled.

Two hours since he'd gotten back from seeing Rose—or whatever the hell her real name was—and he was still rattling around his house like a teenager during summer vacation. Nothing appealed. Paperwork left him cold. Brooding and pacing were unconstructive. Sleep was out of the question.

In short, the woman had made him crazy.

He chucked the wood on his scrap pile, tore off his safety glasses and stalked upstairs from the basement. In spite of his absolute certainty that someone like Rose wouldn't be able to work her manipulative womancraft on *him,* he'd fallen for it, for her, for the entire picture. Sucked in by the transparent wiles of a woman he'd taken thorough pains to arm himself against. Not a notch better than Captain Watson's "whipped" police detective, who'd earned Riley's immediate scornful disrespect.

From the second Riley walked into the room, Rose had him off balance. She was twice as beautiful and sexy as he'd imagined, because she was so damn unexpectedly wholesome and natural. Her "innocence" had awakened his tenderness, something he rarely allowed himself to feel toward women. And in that one, heart-cracking moment when tears dripped down her face, he'd wanted to protect her, make sure no other man could ever hurt her. He wanted to give her the safety she needed, the sexual journey she craved, make her *his*. Hell, he'd even kissed her like a real lover.

Riley laughed bitterly. Horseshit, all of it. She'd had him where she wanted him nearly the entire evening. Right up until the moment his fingers pressed against her heat, when the whole act fell apart. When she spread eagerly to receive him, lay back and gave herself over to her own pleasure, grasping greedily for her climax like the seasoned veteran she was.

After that, he couldn't get out of there fast enough. The transition completely blindsided him. For all his training and discipline, he wasn't able to reverse emotional gears nearly as fast as she could. She was an artist, a master, a Jezebel.

Riley stopped in the doorway to the kitchen and clenched his fists. After all those years pushing himself to the limit, sidestepping his father's footprints by ditching Princeton and traveling the world on pennies a day, facing life and death head-on in the military, he had emerged knowing himself inside out. No surprises. He knew what he wanted from his life, knew what made him tick, how far he could be pushed. He knew his entire emotional landscape, inside out.

Until he'd walked into the tacky, overdecorated apartment of one manipulative man-eating bimbo and got chewed up and spit out in the space of an hour.

He slammed his fist against the door. And damn it all to hell, he wanted her still. In the most primal, arrogant, male way possible, a way that shamed him and what he believed. He wanted to own her, master her, control her the way she'd controlled him—a repeat of the horrifying glimpse into his baser instincts when he'd practically forced himself on her. After she'd taunted him with that little-girl kiss on his mouth. For one red-hazed minute, he'd given in to the primitive male need to dominate, pulling back only when he sensed her fear.

Probably the only genuine emotion she'd displayed all evening.

The refrigerator gave a protesting squeak as he yanked it open and stared inside, desperately needing a long cool drink—something to cool his mind, his body, his attitude. But there probably wasn't anything that powerful on the market.

He gulped the last of the orange juice, crumpled the carton, lobbed it into the trash and headed to his bedroom to change clothes, pushing Rose firmly from his mind. He pulled on shorts, pushed Rose firmly from his mind and ran back down to the basement. Exercise would work off his stress, restore some equilibrium.

Warm-up. Stretch. Heavy weights. Squats, lunges, abdominal crunches, push-ups, triceps dips, biceps curls. He immersed himself in the carefully planned, carefully controlled routine, all the familiar patterns, on and on until his muscles shook.

Cool-down. Stretch. Done.

He headed back upstairs, chugged a quart of water, showered, pulled on clean boxers and slid into bed, holding tight to the hard-won discipline over body and mind he'd come to rely on.

Warm air blew over him from the open window, carrying with it the noises and smells of summer in Brookline. The occasional whoosh of a car, the laughter of neighbors walking their dog down Willard Road.

Relax. He cleared his mind, pushed distracting thoughts firmly away. Light. Clean. Heading toward sleep.

The slide into unconsciousness weakened his control, and she came immediately. She stole over him, smiling, whispering, vulnerable and secretive, then taunting, teasing, sliding her soft lips down his belly, cupping him between his legs, lowering her mouth to suck him dry.

Riley jerked awake and stared at the ceiling, muscles clenched, his erection like granite under the sheet.

Damn.

The cooling breeze dwindled; humidity climbed into the room. Perspiration coated his body. He flipped over onto his stomach, hands at his temples as if to block out the picture his dream had implanted, and found himself pushing rhythmically into the mattress, instinctively trying to ease the aching pressure behind his groin.

No.

He flipped back and restarted his relaxation routine,

instructing the seductive images to leave him alone, instructing his brain to banish Rose and leave him in peace.

The air thickened; stubborn, insistent, the images flickered again through his mind, making relaxation efforts useless. He put his hand up to his face, wishing her scent still lingered on his fingers, remembering the way she'd arched her slender body, offering her wet center as if she wanted it to belong to him more than to her.

Hell.

He reached into his boxers, pushed them down and out of the way with the other hand. She'd won, damn her. He couldn't even resist her memory.

His orgasm came almost immediately, long, shuddering, shockingly intense. He lay still until his breathing slowed, then got out of bed and stood in the shower again, willing the warm, soothing flow of the water to cleanse the woman from his mind.

Enough. Time to stop wallowing in his mistake and start over. He flung back the shower curtain, pulled a towel over and around himself, caught a glimpse of his face in the mirror and almost laughed.

Regroup, Riley. He finished drying himself and arranged his towel neatly on the rack, grinning and shaking his head. She'd roughed him up. Yeah, but he'd been roughed up before. He'd grown complacent, thinking he knew everything that could rattle him and what it would take to adjust to or avoid the reaction. Rose was merely something new to get used to. Like every crisis, the episode would soon settle into perspective. His mission was to find stolen art, not play Tame the Hedonist.

Before the next visit he'd be doubly prepared, tied

tight enough to cut off all emotional circulation. He'd focus on the fact that she was a manipulative bitch who polished off grown men at snack time. Focus on finding the portrait as fast as possible so he could leave this sick situation behind. The woman could have only as much power over him as he gave her.

From now on, he would give her none.

ROSE BURROWED DOWN under her blankets, dimly aware that it must be morning and she was in Maine now, in Slate's cabin, but unwilling to face waking up. Life was so deliciously warm and simple alone in bed. You were either asleep or you weren't. It wasn't until you stepped out that decisions had to be made, appearances kept up, responsibilities shouldered or put off, relationships developed or severed. Not that she'd be facing the same kind of unpleasantness here that she'd left in Boston.

Last night—or rather, early this morning—she'd climbed out of Slate's pickup into the most total darkness she'd ever encountered, and taken in a rapturous lungful of the light, fragrant air. At that moment the break-in, the thugs and the probably traitorous Senator Mason seemed like a nightmarish part of a long-ago dream. She had Slate to thank for that.

He'd taken her plight—and the necessary steps to escape swiftly and unseen—in stride, as if he did this kind of thing all the time. Of course, being a high school teacher, he wasn't likely to. At the station, when his friend didn't arrive on the appointed train, he'd taken Rose boldly out the front entrance, goons be damned. They'd run down the steps to the T and on a riotous trip—subway lines, cabs and on foot—until they were laughing, breathless and sure no one had been able to follow them. From there they'd retrieved Slate's truck and a few of his personal items, and hit the highway.

She owed him a tremendous amount. Quite possibly her life.

How you went about repaying someone for saving your life was beyond her realm of experience, but she knew a thing or two about making men happy. Slate wouldn't regret helping her.

The metallic groan and clank of the wood-burning stove closing came clearly into her bedroom. Slate had lit a fire last night to take the unlived-in chill out of the house. He must have lit another to warm up the morning.

She yawned and sat up reluctantly, taking in the plain pine walls lit dappled yellow by the sun streaming in through the trees; it had been so dark last night she hadn't thought to close the shades. A chickadee sang outside and a startled squirrel scolded; waves swished quietly down in the bay.

Rose grinned and shook her head. *Toto, we are not in Cambridge anymore.* No Ted's TV Repair trucks, no tapped phone lines. No phone lines at all, from what Slate had told her, nor electricity. Roughing it in supreme comfort.

She slid out of bed and pulled on one of the sundresses she'd brought, the sweater she'd worn last night and her heeled sandals. It was lucky Slate had proved himself attracted, when he'd first offered to buy her a drink at the station, because the blonde, sundress look was all she had with her. She pulled on her wig, tucked her hair carefully inside and applied her makeup. All the available armor at hand.

At the door to the bedroom she paused. Two

weeks, twenty-four hours a day in the middle of no-where with an appealing, complex man she wanted to make glad he'd chosen to protect her. The longest date of her life. She took a deep breath and lifted the door's iron latch.

Ready. Set. Go.

The sunny living room startled her with its drab appearance. Funny how it had looked so charming and magical last night. Maybe because last night she'd felt like a caterpillar embraced in a safe cocoon after days dodging ravenous birds.

A greenish-gray woven grass rug, chewed in several places, probably by mice, covered the pine floorboards. A few seashells lay on cobweb-covered windowsills; a few dusty works of children's art, probably Slate's, hung crookedly on the walls. The floor was clean—obviously Slate had kept up with the sweeping—but the house seemed devoid of something. Devoid of life, devoid of the memories and charm a cabin like this should be full of.

Slate poked his head in from the kitchen and grinned. "Good morning. Breakfast is almost ready."

She pulled her body up straight, tilted her chin and smiled. "Thanks, I'm starving."

He ran his eyes over her. Rose stiffened, unable to read his expression. Approval? Disapproval? She could have sworn it was the latter, but he was good at hiding his feelings. A little too good for her peace of mind. He'd had her on edge a good deal last night. On the one hand, he'd acted as if he was making up the rules for their escape as he went along. Underneath, though, she sensed an edge of purposeful power that fascinated her, as if he'd climbed a lot of forbidding peaks in his life, fought many gruesome battles, regularly peered into the jaws of death without so much as a flinch.

She stepped into the kitchen, noting the same blandness, the lack of personal touches that would have proclaimed the cabin as belonging to Slate's family. "Can I help?"

"No, thanks, it's all under control." He spooned out two portions of scrambled eggs, added strips of bacon and an English muffin that had been toasting on a metal rack set over the gas burner. "Have a seat."

Rose crossed to the dining room, really an L off the side of the kitchen, and sat at one of the set places on the long table. He liked to do things on his own. Didn't like help, though he didn't seem to mind her offering. A take-charge kind of guy; she'd noticed that last night, too. She'd need to lie low while she was here.

He sat across from her at the table. Rose put on an attentive expression and sent over another welcoming smile.

"What would you like to do today, Rose?"

"Well...I'd love for you to show me around a little." He'd like that. Take the lead, play Master of his Domain. Help her over rocks and around fallen trees. Put his coat over the mud puddles. Men like him ate that stuff up.

"I'll have to get you something else to wear. There's still some stuff my mom kept up here that I haven't gotten rid of yet. She died recently." He cleared his throat and shoveled in a mouthful of eggs.

Rose nodded, her heart squeezing instinctively. She'd bet anything that mouthful of eggs tasted like sawdust. He was grieving for his mom and didn't want her to see. She immediately turned her attention to her own breakfast. A take-charge guy who hated showing his emotions. Fairly typical, after all. She knew what to do, though she'd never had to do it around-the-clock.

They finished breakfast, Rose feeding him questions about the property, the wildlife and the sea. Then Slate went upstairs and brought down clothes that smelled like cedar and a faint flowery cologne. He pushed them at her and turned away to clear the table.

"Let me at least do the dishes." She'd offer; he'd refuse.

He shook his head. "Tomorrow you can help if you want. Go get dressed and we can get started."

She nodded politely, went back to her room and pulled on the clothes, spraying herself with her own perfume so his mom's scent wouldn't bother him. The jeans and flannel shirt were a little big, but they felt wonderful—soft, warm and comfortable. The sneakers fit perfectly. Rose bit her lip. In this getup she'd lose the sundress look that had attracted Slate at the station. She'd have to work harder at keeping her attitude the same: woman in need of rescue. Make sure he felt useful, needed, as if she relied on his strength to keep her going.

She rolled up the pants and the sleeves, then tied the shirttails in a knot at her waist so her skin would be exposed when she bent over. That would have to do. She sighed and walked back to the kitchen. Paying back someone who'd saved your life could be seriously draining. But a small price to pay for safety.

"How's this?" She smiled at Slate a little anxiously, letting him know she cared what he thought of her appearance, wondering if she'd be able to snatch hours here and there to escape and be herself. "Better?"

He put the last dish in the rack and took two steps toward her, hands on his hips, expression grim, indecisive. Rose felt her smile freeze. He wasn't going to want her to totter around the woods in heeled sandals, was he? She'd never make it. Maybe she could manage to twist her ankle, or—

Before she saw him move, his hand shot out to the top of her head, plucked off her wig and tossed it onto the counter. "There."

Rose clapped her hands to her head and stared at him, breath coming fast from the surprise attack. He reached out and smoothed back her bangs, probably a greasy mess after spending yesterday under the wig and all night on a pillow.

"Better now." He gave a short nod, watching her intently, the expression in his blue eyes still unreadable. "Much better."

She nodded in turn, stifling the urge to grab her wig and pull it back on. She felt disoriented and vulnerable with sloppy clothes and her own hair showing, in front of a man. Maybe she'd been wrong about what attracted him. Maybe he preferred the girl-next-door appeal. But then why would he seek out a platinum blonde in heels at the station?

She summoned a smile, more rattled than she wanted him to see. "Okay, I'm ready. Lead the way."

He took a step closer, close enough so that she could smell him, sense his warmth, touch the smooth fabric of his T-shirt under his open shirt with the merest stretch of her hand, if she wanted to. And God help her, she wanted to, with a sudden force that startled her.

"Rose." His voice came out low and husky, as if what he was saying was emotional, and difficult for him. "I think it's only fair to warn you that while you're here, I'm going to try and do something I'm betting no man has ever done to you."

Her jaw dropped; her breath rushed in with a gasp. She tried to think of a response appropriate to what he might want to hear, but her brain wouldn't work, wouldn't transmit anything but awareness of the heat rushing through her body. "What...what is that?"

He bent forward, quirked an eyebrow and grinned. "Find out who the *hell* you are."

5

MELISSA SWUNG her office chair back and forth, dreamily trailing a finger across her keyboard and making a gentle, almost musical rattling sound. She sighed, laid her head back, ran her fingers through her new short hair, stretched her arms wide and idly contemplated the ugliness of office ceilings.

Nearly lunchtime and she'd gotten nothing done. Nothing. Not a thing. Unless you counted working out in meticulous detail several highly sensual episodes starring her and Riley, which she doubted her boss would count. Everything about her job had become invasive and irritating compared to her secret fantasy-come-true.

How she'd lucked into a situation like this with a guy that perfect, she'd never know. It was tempting to use the standard "somebody up there likes me," but since she'd been raised Catholic, it was unlikely her parents' version of God was going out of his way to make her premarital sex life better.

Right now her major challenge was lasting until tomorrow to see him again. She'd bought a magazine with an article entitled "Ten Naughty Ways He Can Drive You Wild," though she'd spent a long time with the cashier, chatting about her excitement over the window-decorating tips in the same issue. Okay, so her inner wild woman was still pretty tightly closeted.

Nine of the ways he could drive her wild she could have thought of herself. The article was obviously written for someone terrified of her own body, catchy title notwithstanding. But the tenth one—well, she'd passed a toy store and gone in impulsively, then found herself purchasing a police kit with handcuffs, wondering what the sweet grandmotherly saleslady would do if she knew what Melissa wanted them for. Chances were she'd never work up the nerve to use them, but just owning them excited her. In fact, just being alive excited her. This was the best—

"Hey! Guess what?"

Melissa started and nearly tipped her chair back. "God, Penny, don't ever do that again. You almost gave me a—"

"Remember those fabulous miniature portraits every museum in the country went nuts over a few years ago?" Penny's head peeked around her door. "My brother Frank, the cop, just told me a new one has surfaced here in Boston. And get this—they think it might be a portrait that Queen Elizabeth allowed Hilliard to paint in her old age. The one they couldn't find that's listed…in his…" Penny gave Melissa a curious look, then slowly raised an eyebrow. "Uh, Melissa?"

"What?" The blush started at Melissa's neck and rose up her face, defying her efforts to suppress it. She had an awful feeling her friend had seen more than she wanted her to.

"Wow." Penny scooted into her office and closed the door behind her. "Whatever you were thinking, let me in on it. If it was half as good as it looked I could use a dose."

"Oh, no, it wasn't anything like that." Melissa made a lame attempt at careless laughter. "I was typing notes for the chairman's speech tonight."

Penny glanced at Melissa's computer screensaver, contentedly swirling colored patterns across the monitor.

Melissa wrinkled her nose. "Okay, so I hit a little dry patch."

"Ha!" Penny folded her arms across her chest. "Looked to me like a big wet patch. What's his name?"

"Whose name?" Melissa blinked innocently, absolutely dying to confess everything. Who wouldn't want to brag about an affair with someone as amazing as Riley? Penny would live off the gossip for weeks.

Penny sighed. "Melissa, I have known you for eight years. During that time you have had maybe one emotion you actually managed to hide from me—when you were afraid I'd hate the male strip-'o-gram you got me for my twenty-fifth birthday. Someone is on your mind, and it ain't a she. Now, give."

Melissa rolled her chair back from its unproductive position in front of the computer and fixed Penny with a blissful smile. "His name is Riley and he's about the most incredible guy I've ever met."

"Now we're getting somewhere." Penny dragged a chair closer, plopped into it and pushed up her glasses. "Riley who?"

Melissa's blissful smile faltered. Had he told her? Had Rose told her? "Riley..."

Penny's mouth dropped. "You don't know?"

"We've only met once. A mutual friend fixed us up."

"And you didn't tell me?"

"It all happened so fast." Melissa gestured helplessly, knowing she couldn't describe what had happened without it sounding unfairly sordid. "She called him and then the next night—"

"Who called him?"

"Rose."

"Rose who?"

Melissa stared blankly at Penny's face, mind churning. Rose…Rose…

"She lives across from me."

"Rose? *That* Rose? The one who dates the Fixodent set? The one you said you thought was in trouble? Who is this guy, some billionaire octogenarian mafioso?"

"No. He's young. Maybe thirty-five. And he's gorgeous. And he's…he's…" She searched for words to describe him, but the only ones that came to mind were *smoldering* and *dangerously erotic,* and she didn't think either of those would sell Penny on the concept. "He's nice."

"He's nice." Penny fixed her with a skeptical glare. "What are you doing, Melissa? Is this that sex-with-a-stranger thing you were talking about?"

"Uh…well, sort of. Only he's not a total stranger."

"No." The skeptical glare grew decidedly more skeptical.

"Well, it's not like I met him in a bar. He's a friend of a friend of Rose's."

"Even Rose doesn't know him?" Penny's voice rose to an outraged squeak.

Melissa twisted uncomfortably. There was no way

she could explain this situation so that it appealed to Penny. "Not that well, no."

"Who *does* know this guy?"

"Rose's friend. Amanda."

Penny leaned forward, right into Melissa's face. "Amanda...who?"

Melissa threw up her hands, feeling like a fourteen-year-old being interrogated by her mother. "Penny, I don't know. I just know Rose told me Amanda had a sexy friend named Tom, who—"

"You said his name was Riley."

"It is." She took a deep breath and willed herself to be patient. Penny would understand eventually. Maybe by her eightieth birthday. "But his *middle* name is Riley. He—"

"Okay, never mind, I've got it." Penny stood, hands out like a cop stopping traffic. "You go to Rose, whose last name you don't know, who routinely dates icky old men and who you think might be in some kind of trouble, and ask her who you can sleep with. She calls someone you don't know from Eve, someone with no last name, while you're standing there—"

"I was out of the room when she called Amanda. Rose asked me to—" Melissa clamped her mouth shut. If she told Penny that Rose had suggested she go to her own apartment while Rose made the call, Penny would only add it to her absurd soap-opera version of what happened.

"Oh, good! She orders you out of the room, which you do without question, and while you're not there, so we don't know who she *really* called, she gets you a date with her friend's friend Tom aka Riley—guess what, no last name—who shows up at your apartment and—''

"Rose's apartment." Melissa rolled her eyes. This would cook her. "Rose was out."

"Ah, even *better*. He shows up at *her* apartment, and says, oh, by the way, my name isn't Tom, it's Riley, but I still don't have a last name, and you say, 'Great! Let's have sex!'"

"Pretty much." Melissa shrugged as if Penny had described what she did every day of the week. "Except I didn't exactly have sex with him."

Penny sighed. "Not exactly?"

"No. I mean, we did…other things." She shifted in her seat, remembering.

"Other things." Penny's face wrinkled in concern. "Oh, Melissa. This whole thing sounds really creepy to me. I mean, how do you know Rose didn't set you up somehow? Isn't it a little strange that she just happened to find someone for the next night? How many people do you know who would go on a blind sex date?"

"Penny, we're talking guys here."

"Okay, never mind that question." Penny dismissed it with a floppy-wristed wave. "But why the hell would she want you having sex in *her* apartment? Eww."

"I don't know." Melissa made an earnest attempt not to sound as exasperated as she felt. "I thought it was probably smart for him not to know where I live at first."

"Aha!" Penny held up a triumphant finger. "Very true. There is a shred of common sense in you, after all. This is good. We can work with this. We can nurture this. So at the very least this friend of

Amanda—if that's her real name—who's a friend of Rose—no doubt *not* her real name—Tom-slash-Riley—if that is even *close* to his real name—does not know where you live.''

Melissa rolled her eyes. Penny was on a rampage. "Penny…"

"Yes, Melissa? I'm assuming Melissa *is* your real name?"

Something vaguely unpleasant gave a little jolt to Melissa's system. *Melissa is your real name?*

"What's the matter?" Penny blinked at her, not missing one iota. As usual.

"Nothing, really." The vaguely unpleasant feeling began to crystallize into a focused, genuinely unpleasant feeling. "It's just funny—that was what Riley said, 'Melissa is your real name?' Right after he called me…Rose."

"He called you Rose?" Penny threw up her hands. "Why does no one in this untimely adventure have a name they stick to?"

"Well, by mistake. I mean, obviously he knows I'm not her."

Penny put her hands on her hips. "Are you sure Tom-Riley has met Rose?"

"Uh…" Melissa tried to remember everything Rose had said about Tom. The unpleasantness churned into nausea. "Well, I guess she didn't actually say she knew him. No."

"So what the hell happened, Melissa? He showed up thinking you were Rose?"

Melissa grimaced, unwilling to acknowledge the possibility bonking her repeatedly on the head. It couldn't be. Ridiculous. Even though it would explain the way Riley had treated her, as if he thought she was faking her inexperience. And explain why he wanted to know how many men she'd actually slept with. And explain why he was surprised she wanted him there as her teacher, and why he got angry when she kissed him like a little girl, and why he needed to know about all the "other dates" she went on...and on and on.

"It does...explain some things. Like why he couldn't get over how innocent I seemed, for one." Melissa clutched her stomach. She was either going to be sick or just feel like this for the rest of the day, which was almost as bad.

Penny helped matters not at all by bursting into laughter. "God, I would have given anything to be a fly on the wall during that date. You being all sweet and nervous and him trying to figure out what happened to the sex goddess he expected."

"Shut up, Penny. This isn't funny. I'm supposed to see him again tomorrow."

"Well, call him up and..." Penny's laughter died when she saw Melissa's face. "Don't tell me. You don't have his number."

Melissa shook her head. This was quite probably the most humiliating day of her life. Worse than when Patrick Corey threw up all over the prom dress she'd spent three months making. Worse than when she'd walked in on her favorite college professor having sex—with Melissa's boyfriend. Worse than when Bill had told her she'd never excite him as much as Michelle Pfeiffer. Worse than—

"Wait a second, though." Penny frowned. "Wouldn't Rose have said, 'Gee, Tom-Riley, I have this friend named Melissa I want you to have sex with?' I mean, I can't really imagine a scenario where she would have left that part out.''

"Me, neither." Melissa slouched down in her seat. So maybe it wasn't the case. Unless...*oh, no.* "I bet it was because Rose knew he'd come for sure if it was to meet her. No man would turn Rose down. The woman could arouse a homosexual eunuch.''

"Oh, geez, Melissa. Ostriches have more sexual self-esteem than you do. That makes about zero sense. In fact only one thing in this entire mess is clear.'' Penny shook her finger sharply in Melissa's face. "You'd be a total idiot to see that guy again.''

"I know...."

Wild denial rose in her, sharp and strong. The strange, crazy darkness swelled and grew, like the gloriously fierce, panicky prelude to an impossible-odds battle. She wasn't going to give him up. Even if it meant seeing someone who might have zero connections to people she knew and trusted. She'd spent her entire life on the right side of the tracks. This was her time to branch out.

After the way she'd fallen apart in his arms, she was convinced Riley held the key to unleashing and naming whatever primal creature lurked inside her. Her time with him could be the beast's only chance to prowl and explore its savage existence before the inevitable white picket fence of Melissa's future closed around her and forced the creature's retreat.

She'd see Riley again. Tell him she wasn't Rose, and see if he'd agree to continue their arrangement anyway. He'd obviously been aroused by their last encounter—it wasn't like the idea would repulse him. In fact, considering how confused he'd been when he was thinking she was Rose, he'd probably be relieved she was just plain old Melissa. Sweet, wholesome and innocent. As simple and straightforward as a nice girl could be who happened to be burning with wild demon mating lust.

She nodded seriously to Penny, the heat still storming inside her. "You're right. I'd be an idiot to see him again."

And idiocy was going to feel damn good.

RILEY FINISHED HIS morning coffee, picked up the phone to call his sister, and heard the stuttering dial tone indicating he had voice mail. He left a brief message on Karen's machine, telling her he'd pick up Leo in the morning for their visit to the aquarium, then dialed the voice mail retrieval number. A female voice told him the message had come in at two that morning—shortly before he'd gotten home from tracking a missing person and fallen straight into bed.

Slate's voice came on the line, crackling indistinctly. "Sorry to call so late. Rose is with me in Maine. No portrait found on her yet. Happy hunting."

The line beeped. A mechanical voice urged him to delete or save the message.

Riley closed his eyes, trying to gain control of the crazy, irrational jealousy churning his insides. He'd spent the entire day yesterday not thinking about Rose. Not thinking about their adventure tonight and what it might entail. How she would look; how she would feel. He even hadn't thought of a few possibilities for their encounter. And while he was doing all that non-thinking, Slate had her. In the middle of nowhere. All to himself.

Son of a bitch.

Riley pressed the button to delete the message and

put the phone back into its cradle, resisting the urge to slam it down. Who would Rose become for Slate, to entice him and get past his restraint where women were concerned? His perfect girl-next-door match? Exotic woman of experience to offset his boyish charm? Was she smiling sweetly? Suggestively? Letting show occasional glimpses of leg or breast to drive him wild?

Riley forced his muscles to loosen, tried to deepen and slow his breathing. He should be feeling sorry for his friend, not wanting to punch him out. Slate had already been intrigued, listening on the phone tap when Rose made arrangements with that Tom guy. Chances were good he'd get his heart punctured by her steel-trap artifice.

Relax. Riley went into his living room and sat on the carpet, closed his eyes, concentrated again on his breathing and waited until his mind cleared, his anger receded and calm control took over.

Okay.

So Rose was out of the picture. Which left her apartment wide-open. Jake Allston's people wouldn't dare send someone in with the cops monitoring the building, but if Riley went in alone and searched, he'd become an obvious target for whoever wanted the portrait. Becoming an obvious target was not his favorite activity. People like Jake Allston tended to hold grudges; latch on, pit bull style, to the desire to eliminate, and not stop until the job was done.

Calculate. Slate had left the message at 2:00 a.m. So he couldn't have left Boston later than eight or nine o'clock yesterday. Knowing Slate, he hadn't been followed; whoever was tracking Rose wouldn't know she'd gone out of state. Riley glanced at his watch. Seven-thirty. At this hour, it was conceivable someone watching the building could be fooled into thinking Rose was back home, asleep.

Her bed was against the wall, out of sight from the window. He could go in and pretend he was talking to her. Gesture. Laugh. Bend down for a kiss. The FBI would have a bug in the room, but he doubted Allston's people had set up anything more than a visual stakeout. He could pretend he was getting clothes from her dresser, food from her refrigerator, cooking breakfast, wandering around the room, occasionally out of sight—all the while searching.

Best possible scenario, he could find the portrait this morning and get this entire episode over with before his meeting with Captain Watson, and later with Ted Barker, FBI.

Worst possible scenario, he'd have to get Rose back from Maine and resume their ridiculous charade, knowing Slate might have already had her.

Riley pushed away the jolt of rage that came with that picture and went out to his car. He drove to Cambridge calmly, purposefully, convincing his mind to accept finding the portrait in the next hour as a certainty. Around the corner from Rose's apartment, he parked, then strode across the Cambridge Common and into her building, keeping focused on the task, not allowing himself to think about what had happened the last time he was here.

Concentrate.

He rode the elevator up, stepped out onto her floor, turned resolutely toward her apartment and stopped. Rose. Striding down the hall toward him, slender, vibrant, eyes wide, lips parted in surprise.

What the—

"Rose—Melissa. What the hell are you doing here?"

She held out the hand that had jumped to her chest at the sight of him and raised her eyebrows. "Uh...I *live* here. What the hell are *you* doing here?"

Riley stared. Stared harder. She shifted under his scrutiny. A blush there was no way she could have manufactured spread up her face.

Rose is with me, in Maine.

Melissa is your real name?

He closed his eyes against a giddy rush of relief.

She wasn't Rose.

He hadn't lost his mind. Wasn't just another male lemming driven to mental suicide. She wasn't Rose. He could have kissed her, except he had some enormous lies to come up with to explain what the hell he was doing here, and he had to find out exactly how this woman fit into the picture. Right now all he knew about her was that she wasn't Rose and she wanted to have sex with him.

"I wanted to see you. I hoped to catch you before..." he gestured to her beige suit "...before you left for work."

"Oh?"

"I would have called, but I didn't have your number." He cleared his throat. *Think, Riley, think.* "I wanted to ask you..."

She winced and gave him a sheepish half smile. "I think I know what you wanted to ask."

He felt his expression start to freeze and forced it to remain neutral. "You do."

"Yes." She moved her shoulders uncomfortably, as if she were trying to shrug off something that was bothering her. "You want to ask why if I'm Rose, I told you my name is Melissa, and why I was so…confusing.''

He wanted to laugh at the understatement. "You certainly were confusing."

"I only *seemed* confusing because…" She bit her lip and looked at him apprehensively. "I'm not Rose. I wasn't pretending to be her—I didn't realize that's what you must have thought until yesterday, when I started putting some pieces together, and then I had no way to reach you and explain."

"I see." He looked carefully for any sign of lying and found none. She was utterly convincing. "You didn't know I was expecting Rose?"

"No." She fidgeted and didn't meet his eyes, but he sensed only chagrin, not subterfuge. "Rose set this up. I don't know why she didn't tell you. She might have figured if you thought you were meeting her you'd be more likely to come."

"I didn't come, as you recall."

"You—" She caught his smile and laughed nervously at the joke.

Riley relaxed further. "You don't think you were enough of a draw to get me here?"

She rolled her eyes. "Well, I don't know. Not next to *her,* certainly. I was probably crazy to go to her in the first place to recommend someone, but I figured she'd know lots of men, and…well, you know the rest.''

Riley nodded, keeping his gleeful satisfaction in check. He knew the rest. The Feds could check Melissa out to be sure she was as innocent as she seemed, but he was betting there wasn't so much as a parking ticket on her record. In the meantime, with Rose safely out of the way, Melissa would provide the perfect cover for continuing the search of Rose's place. They'd both get what they wanted.

"I hope…that won't make a difference, that I'm not Rose. I mean, if you want to stop seeing me, I'd understand."

He stepped closer, smiled, reached out and ran his finger across her lips. "It sure as hell wasn't your name I was attracted to the other night."

She inhaled and exhaled quickly, a little gasp that sounded as if he'd managed to turn her on just with his words and one small touch. Fresh-faced and proper in that professional suit, getting rosy and wet from hearing his voice. He suppressed a smile, leaned forward, kissed her, drawing his tongue lightly across her mouth to tease her.

She made a tiny sexy sound, then moved forward and caught his lower lip between her teeth in a brief, gentle bite.

The contact jolted him with unexpected erotic electricity. He fisted the hands that were about to reach for her, and drew away, surprised at his reaction. What was that? He liked women who'd been around, who could match his sexual experience and cynical attitude. For all her bravado in wanting a sexual odyssey, Melissa was hardly that kind.

"So I'll see you tonight?" He brought himself to heel, kept his voice casual.

"Yes." She nodded rapidly, flushed and beaming, and glanced at her watch. "I better run or I'll be late."

He accompanied her down the hall to the elevator, back in emotional balance. "Do you want to meet at Rose's place again? I'm assuming she's out of town."

"Oh, I didn't—well, sure. It sort of…fits the occasion. I don't think she'd mind."

He pushed the button for the elevator and followed her inside. Perfect. He didn't even have to come up with a reason they should meet there. The investigation was being handed to him on a slender, beige-suited dish.

He followed Melissa into the building's foyer and glanced behind her head at the panel housing the door buzzers, to find out her last name and which apartment she lived in, so the Feds could run a check.

He'd barely taken in the first two names when Melissa backed firmly against the wall, door in one hand, head covering the panel.

"How do you feel about women opening doors for you?" She gestured to the street and met his eyes calmly.

"Liberated." He stepped ahead of her, wondering if she'd deliberately tried to obscure his view, and paused on the sidewalk breathing the cool morning air, tinged with exhaust fumes, until she joined him.

"Have a nice day at work, dear." He leaned forward and kissed her forehead.

She laughed. "You'll have dinner waiting when I get home, I trust."

"Something nice and hot." He winked at her. "You want to choose the menu or should I?"

"I have some ideas." She smiled shyly. "Maybe you could come up with half the meal?"

"I think I could do that." He almost laughed. How the hell could he ever have thought this woman anything but what she appeared?

She swayed toward him, then seemed to lose her

nerve and gave a little wave with her fingers. "See you tonight."

Riley watched her walk down the block, grinning with pleasure. Instead of agonizing over becoming ensnared by someone like Rose, he was on top of the case, in control, and dealing with a lovely, uncomplicated woman who did beautiful things to a mini-skirted suit, and whose idea of kinky sex was probably doing it with the lights on.

He meandered in the opposite direction, turned the corner and waited a few minutes, then doubled back to her building and went inside to check the buzzer panel so he could pass her name along to the Feds.

B. Joyce, S. Shute, H. Harriman, A. Faloud, R. Sheppard…M. Rogers. Riley grinned and pushed the buzzer for the hell of it.

Bingo.

He'd wasted incredible energy on the self-torture of uncertainty. Now, in a few hours, with the FBI machine behind him, the no-longer-mysterious Melissa Rogers would be a wide-open book.

He left the building and strode down the street toward his car, chuckling in satisfaction.

And tonight he'd get to read between her lines.

6

MELISSA LAY ON HER BACK on Rose's bed, wiggling her bare feet. She'd decided not to wear shoes for her date with Riley tonight, because it was always sort of awkward taking shoes off. Well, shoes weren't bad, but taking socks off was decidedly unsexy. Especially if you were wearing knee-highs and the guy took your pants off first, and there you were with half your legs too brown and a big dark band under your knee, still trying to act sexy while you felt like a bag lady.

She closed her eyes, trying to still the inane chatter in her brain. There were more important things to worry about. Like whether she was risking her life or health or sanity offering handcuffs to a guy she didn't know. Here she was, planning to trust him with her body, but she'd jumped to avoid meeting him at her own place, and instinctively tried to hide her last name and apartment number when he'd been scanning the building's buzzers.

Obviously, for all her bravado, she hadn't quite made up her mind about him.

She shifted and stretched on the bed. Enough. Been there, worried about that. Odds were huge he was just what he seemed: an incredibly sexy, emotionally closed man willing to fulfill her every desire. The fact that she'd found him on the first try was like buying only one lottery ticket in a lifetime and hitting the jackpot. Her time would be much better spent imagining herself shackled to the bed, completely at Riley's mercy.

The dark excitement unfurled in her body, wrapped her in warmth. She put her hands over her eyes, as if ashamed of her own longing. *Okay, admit it, Melissa.* The truth. That sense of danger, that tiny uncertainty about him was a total turn-on. To be bound, immobile, and totally in the control of a man she knew next to nothing about, who fulfilled her every fantasy of what it was to be female—well, it made her wild.

So she was a bestial slut from hell. But she'd be the *best* gosh darn bestial slut from hell she knew how to be. At least while the adventure lasted.

Melissa giggled and turned over, still not quite able to believe this was happening to her. She'd spent a hyperordinary Saturday, grocery shopping, doing errands, cleaning her apartment, greeting and chatting with people she knew, all the while aware of the crazy secret burning inside her, a secret no one in a million years would expect of sweet innocent Melissa.

She pushed herself off the bed and prowled the apartment. He'd be here any minute. Half of her damn well couldn't wait. The rest of her was nearly shaking with nerves.

Welcome to the wonderful world of Melissa Rogers. Pick a personality and wait your turn.

His knock sounded at the door. Melissa's heart leaped into warp speed. Maybe the handcuffs should wait. Maybe she'd do better with her ice cube fantasy, or honey. Or maybe just a nice conversation. Or a movie. Or Bible study.

He knocked again. *Okay, Melissa, front and center.* She turned determinedly, ran her fingers through her hair, adjusted her white, sleeveless, not-yet-hopelessly-wrinkled linen top and black rayon draw-string pants and went to answer.

"Hello, Melissa." Riley smiled down at her, dark and handsome, the definition of virility in khakis and a white, short-sleeved shirt with a teal pinstripe. From his fingers hung a small paper shopping bag that immediately drew Melissa's wary gaze.

He winked. "Dessert."

"Oh, nice." She grinned weakly. As long as it wasn't molded rubber...

"Come in." She gestured him into the apartment, her Sweet and Proper side taking firm control in a rush of crazy nerves. Once they got...going she would be fine. Of course she would. But how did you *get* going?

"Would you like a drink?" She didn't really want one, though the tiniest buzz of alcohol might help her relax. But she couldn't help offering, since she appeared to have morphed into Miss Manners the minute she laid eyes on him.

"Sure." He glanced around the apartment, taking everything in as if he'd never been there before. Then he did it again, this time a slow circular perusal of the room, examining everything...except her.

Melissa escaped to the kitchen. *Oh, no.* Something was distracting him. Their easy camaraderie of the morning was missing. He was even doing that one-word-sentence thing again. If anything, he seemed more of a stranger than before she'd met him. She sloshed Irish whiskey over ice, scoffing at the cubes in the glass. Who did she think she was, Linda Lovelace? Forget the ice. Forget the honey. Forget the handcuffs. It would take all her nerve to suggest they sit on the same couch.

She brought the drinks back into the living room, seething with frustration. Riley was bent over Rose's bookcase, engrossed in an apparently fascinating study of her reading habits.

"Irish whiskey okay?" Her voice came out as chilly as the ice in the drinks.

He turned immediately and walked toward her, holding her eyes with a magnetic half smile that deepened the groove in his right cheek and lifted a tiny corner of her despair. Okay, if he'd come up with a complete sentence, she could sit on the couch with him.

He emptied his glass in one gulp and set it down on Rose's coffee table. "Thanks."

Melissa gritted her teeth. "Were we thirsty?"

A sexy grin spread across his face; he shook his head slowly. "No. Impatient. Come here, Melissa."

Impatient. For her. She stepped toward him, her insides beginning to melt into a nice heated indoor pool, wondering how he could make "come here" sound like sex-in-the-making instead of a stupid macho come-on.

He took her drink and set it on a nearby end table, put his hands on her shoulders and turned her away from him. Melissa stood waiting for who knew what, her breathing shallow, body trembling idiotically. His mouth settled on the side of her neck, warm and gentle, sending shivers dancing over her skin. The buttons down the back of her blouse tugged and gave way, inevitably, slowly, one by one. The linen loosened around her body; she put her arms down and bent slightly forward so the top fell to her waist.

No question. When he was like this, the man made her want to get naked.

Riley turned her back around to face him and stepped away, smiling down at her lacy, beige cotton bra. Melissa's joyous transformation into Sex Goddess of the Universe came to a screeching halt. She crossed her arms in front of her and glared. "What is so funny?"

"Not funny. Beautiful." He retrieved the bag he'd brought in with him and handed it to her. "But try this. I want to see if it fits."

Melissa opened the bag which, thank goodness, was too light for anything motorized, and pulled out a scarlet lace bra and matching thong panties.

Oh my... She'd never worn anything like this in her life. A *red* bra? She glanced at Riley, face flaming, and got a good eyeful of what a man looks like when he thinks a woman is too chicken to wear sexy underwear.

She lifted her chin and paraded to the painted floral privacy screen Rose had set up across one corner of her studio. *Challenge accepted.* She shed her clothes, hands shaking crazily, and pulled the micropanties on.

The thong was less uncomfortable than she thought it would be, and loose enough so the sides didn't dig into the softness of her hips and make her silhouette lumpy. The bra was too small—thanks, Riley—but better than if it had been huge and made her breasts look wistful and lost.

She studied herself in the mirror Rose had stationed on the wall, probably for checking herself out in exactly such outfits. *Hmm.* From the Melissa perspective, she looked like plain old Melissa dressed up in a sexy outfit, but maybe to him she'd look exotically enticing.

A *thwunk* sounded from the other side of the screen. Melissa frowned and listened intently. A soft swish, and another bump. What the heck was Riley doing out there? She really, really hoped he wasn't setting up some kind of sexual trapeze set.

She went to step back into the room, and her bravery went AWOL for the second time in twenty minutes. Call her a wimp, but she wasn't up to strutting around in tiny underwear in front of a fully-clothed stranger. Her eyes lit on a shawl draped over the folding chair in the corner; she snatched it up and wrapped the silky material around her like a strapless gown.

So she was chicken. Fricassee her.

She counted to three, barged back into the room and caught sight of Riley rising from a crouch next to the rear of Randstetler's tin-can-giraffe sculpture.

Melissa glanced surreptitiously around the room. No trapeze. Nothing too strange unless she started wondering if Riley had overly fond feelings for Mr. Giraffe. She gestured to the shawl. "I've got on the…things under here. They fit."

His brow lifted in skeptical amusement. "Prove it."

She summoned all her nerve and found it didn't meet the amount required to drop the shawl and stand there in front of him in next-to-nothing lingerie. "I can't. Not like this. Not like I'm a…cow at an auction house."

He chuckled, picked up the drink he'd taken from her earlier, and walked closer until he stood in front of Rose's bed. "I don't want you to do anything you

don't want to. We can take this at whatever pace suits
you. Okay?"

More than one sentence. Lots of words. Melissa
nodded happily. A warm and comforting feeling came
over her, as if he'd strung up a safety net beneath her,
so if she stumbled on this crazy tightrope adventure,
she wouldn't splat on the pavement. How many psycho pervert killers would say something so nice? Her
daring rose, along with the excitement engendered by
his dark intense gaze, measuring her reaction.

She let the shawl drop.

Riley froze, her drink in his hand, eyes going over
her minutely. "Nice."

The word came out in a slightly husky tone that
told her just possibly he thought it was very *very* nice.

That was all the license her inner bestial slut from
hell needed. Her courage grew, blossomed, catapulted
her into a sexual confidence she'd never felt with Bill
or any other man. She walked to Riley, put her hands
to his shoulders and lifted her face, hungry for the
taste of his mouth and the tender, passionate way he'd
kissed her before.

He did kiss her, but only once, all too briefly, then
took her shoulders and sat her on the edge of the bed.
"Tell me what you want me to do."

Everything. Okay, not *everything.* No handcuffs.
Not yet. But if Kim Basinger could take an ice bath,
so could she.

"Ice." Melissa pointed to the drink in his hands
and gestured to her body. "All over me. I want to see
how it feels."

He gave her a quizzical look, then fished a piece
of ice out of her drink and held it to her lips. She

opened for him and tasted, savoring the hot burn of whiskey and the cold burn of ice.

He dipped the ice again, held it for her to suck, and moved closer so his body seemed to be above and all around her. He put the glass to her lips and tipped forcefully so whiskey trickled down the sides of her mouth, dripped onto her chest and rolled down into the red bra in a cold, fiery stream.

Melissa reared back. He followed, tasted the whiskey beside her mouth, pushed her back on the bed and licked the drops from the swell of her breasts in the too-tight bra—leisurely strokes with the tip of his tongue on her wet skin. His hands came around to unhook her bra; she felt her breasts released from the confining material, heavy and free. With the release, the last of her inhibitions left, skulked out of the room like the party-poopers they were.

"You're beautiful." He slid his hands over her breasts, then retrieved more ice from the glass next to the bed and pressed it to her neck, slid the cube gently down and over her nipple. The burn of the ice was exquisite; his touch, his nearness, even better. He ran the ice over to her other breast, watching her with an almost unbearable intensity.

"Do you like that?"

"Yes." Her voice came out a breathless whisper that made his eyes darken further.

He kept the ice on its erotic journey, cold drips running down her sides, warmed by her body before they dropped onto the bed. His other hand slid down her stomach, found the thong panties and pulled in a regular rhythm that drew them tight over her wet center, then released. Tighten, release, tighten, release.

Melissa's breath came in slow, irregular pants. She

shivered and burned in a hot-cold swirl of sensation. Through it all Riley watched her, invaded her cocoon of ecstasy with his stare. What did he see? What was he looking for?

He was in the way. She closed her eyes, reached to turn his head away. She wanted this to stay physical, stay pure and erotic. Too much awareness of him, of his strength and magnetic presence, interfered with the fabulous sensations he was making her body feel. It could turn this beautiful, primal moment into a complicated emotional experience.

"Don't watch me."

"I have to watch you." He seemed to struggle even to whisper the words. "You have no idea…"

She made a helpless gesture of protest, her accelerating rush into oblivion interrupted, defeated. The rapidly melting ice stopped in the valley between her breasts, then made a slow descent down her stomach, over her navel, leaving a cold, wet trail. He pulled the red lace aside and slid the now-tiny piece down over her heat, making her gasp and laugh a little. Not quite what she expected. "It's cold."

"You thought it would be otherwise?" His voice was gentle, teasing, as he slid the hard, slippery sliver up and down between her legs. "How does it feel?"

Melissa stifled a shiver. "Like sex with Frosty the Snowman."

He laughed, a real laugh that seemed to surprise even him, and held up empty dripping fingers. "I'm afraid he's…gone."

"Frosty, no!" Melissa clapped a hand to her chest. "It's all my fault. But I got so tired of sex in the deep freeze."

Riley laughed again and shook his head, ran his

hands down her body. "You are a fun date. And at the moment a chilly one."

She pushed aside her pleasure at his compliment and blinked sweetly as if she was going to ask him for a glass of water. "Want to warm me up?"

His grin turned wicked. He climbed up on the bed, straddled her on his knees and started unbuttoning his shirt. "I think I can do that."

Melissa rose to her elbows, wanting to touch him, take her turn exploring his body. "Let me help."

"I've got it." He undid the last button and tossed the shirt aside. Melissa drew her hands down his chest and over his waist, then lay back, uninhibited and happy, eager for the weight of his magnificent torso, the hard press of him on top of her, the hot bulge of him between her legs, then the intimate joining of their bodies.

Instead, he leaned forward, supporting his weight on his arms, and moved his chest lightly down her body, following the trail of warmth with slow, lazy kisses.

Melissa lay back and closed her eyes, trying to concentrate on the rough brush of his hair against her skin and the smooth heat of his mouth, distracted by her irrational disappointment. Of course he wasn't just going to lie on top of her and do it. That's exactly what she didn't want, what she'd *told him* she didn't want. This was an adventure—only the unexpected.

He paused with his face between her thighs, then ran his tongue slowly along the length of her, reheating her chilled sex and bringing her lapsed erotic charge sizzling back to life.

"Oh gosh— I've never— Bill wouldn't— Oh gosh." The words came out breathless and silly in the silence, but she didn't care. He took his time stroking her with his tongue, bending now and then to close his lips and suck firmly over her pleasure.

Melissa held on desperately to her control, fireworks shooting through her body, wanting to hold off, wanting to see what he'd do next, wanting to feel like this just for a few more minutes…or hours… Or days would be fine, too.

He slid one finger inside her, keeping up the rhythm with his tongue, then two fingers, then pulled the thong up hard and tight into her backside, and she was gone, pushed over the edge into a burning burst of delight. She clutched his head, strained to hold on to the moment, push it higher, then pulsed into inevitable ecstasy….

And slowly came down. To lie sated and stupid and dreamy on the pillow, completely unable and totally unwilling to move. Having a fling was the best freaking idea she'd ever had.

"How did *that* feel?" He pushed up and sat on his knees between her legs.

"I think I could live with that." She stretched like the major wanton babe she'd just become, and glanced at his straining pants. "What about you?"

He put a gentle hand on her stomach. "This is your adventure."

"Yes, but I don't want to have *all* the fun." She struggled to sit up. Why didn't he ever let her do anything for him?

"Believe me." He pushed her back down and kissed her inner thigh. "I'm having fun."

"Yes, but—"

"Want to do it again? Or some other way?" He kissed her other thigh, then gently between her legs.

Again? "Uh...I don't think I can this soon."

"Ever tried?"

"Well, not with—I mean..." She rolled her eyes. Like she was really going to share her solo sexual experiences with someone who could have women lining up outside his door with a snap of his fingers. "I just can't yet."

"Okay. No problem." He climbed off the bed and knelt on the floor next to her.

Melissa frowned. What was with this guy? He didn't take his pants off and he didn't go horizontal?

"Riley, no offense, but I feel a little like a science experiment alone on this bed."

For a weird second his features froze, and she was terrified that by wanting to lie with him she'd broken one of the Laws of Casual Sex that everyone knew but her.

"You're awfully far away, is all."

He nodded and stretched out next to her, lying somewhat stiffly, like an adolescent boy who was scared of what he might do. Melissa hesitated, then pushed up against his side and wrapped his arm around her. To hell with his neuroses. This was her fantasy. The ice cubes might not have gone so well, but she'd risked hell and humiliation to get him here, she'd survived the first round and now she wanted it all.

To her relief, he pulled her to him and kissed her temple. "What do you want to do when you're ready?"

Melissa sighed. Some women might be able to toss off requests like, "You know, Riley, it'd be swell if you'd spread honey all over my body and lick it off," but she was pretty damn sure she'd mess it up.

"Have you ever, I mean, well, spread honey all over someone—a woman—well, I mean, of *course* a woman, not like you wouldn't be with a...well, have you?"

She hid her face in his shoulder and groaned silently. For a horrible second she thought he wasn't going to answer. Not that she could blame him. She wasn't quite sure what she'd said herself.

"Why are you doing this, Melissa?"

Her stomach dropped. "You think the honey sounds stupid."

"No." He lifted her face so she had to look at him. "I think it sounds very sexy. But why do you want sex like this, in a vacuum?"

Melissa bristled. "You don't think women can want sex without involvement?"

"I'm not talking about women, I'm talking about you."

"Why do *you* do it?"

"Because it's who I am." He gave a casual wave, as if everyone who had half a brain would know that. "But I don't sense it's who you are, not in quite the same way."

Melissa stifled her irritation. What the hell did he know about her after an hour and a half? "I just want some fun before I'm married."

"Why don't you think you'll marry someone who can do everything you ever dreamed of?"

"Because." She shook her head emphatically. "It wouldn't be the same. He'd know the real Melissa too well."

He tucked his chin down and looked at her quizzically. "The real Melissa?"

"Yes. The woman you have in bed with you right

now isn't really me. She's a personality I want to try on for fun. My evil twin.''

"I see. And who is the real Melissa?"

"Well..." Melissa searched his eyes for signs he was making fun of her, and was relieved and slightly incredulous to find none. "The real Melissa wears suits and is polite and proper all the time. A sweet sexless woman who never gave her parents a single day of anxious worry. A woman who wants to marry a nice, responsible, supportive man and settle down with two kids and a minivan. That's the real me. I'm not unhappy with that, I just want to try something else right now, while I can."

He chuckled. "Tell me more about this evil woman I'm in bed with. She intrigues me."

Melissa rolled away and stared at the ceiling, absurdly grateful for his easy acceptance of what must sound like lunatic rambling. She'd never talked about this strange split she'd been aware of for so long, for fear of being firmly shoved into psychoanalysis. "Sometimes I get this feeling, almost like anger—no, rage, really—and I want to do crazy, irresponsible things."

"Like?"

"Like dress in black leather, spike my hair and walk into a bar alone with an enormous 'F— you' attitude. Jump out of an airplane. Yell back at the movie screen. Be astonishingly rude to people who deserve it. Quit my job, say to hell with salary and benefits, and travel around the world on whatever's in my pocket."

"That I've done."

"Which?"

"Ditched my life and traveled around the world."

"No kidding." She pushed up on her elbow to watch his face. "When?"

"When I dropped out of Princeton."

Melissa gaped at him. The fantasy stud of her life went to Princeton? She suddenly pictured him at age eighteen, earnestly toting around a heavy backpack, discussing Kant with a bespectacled professor, possibly even sporting a pimple or two.

She grimaced and willed the image away.

"That upsets you?" He spoke quietly, watched her face as if he didn't want to miss any nuance of her reaction.

She shrugged sheepishly. "I'm sorry. Apparently I pictured you jumping full-grown out of a *Playgirl* magazine."

"Centerfold Without A Past?" He reached up and playfully pushed her bangs aside, but his eyes stayed serious.

Melissa winced. She sounded like a complete sexist horror. If any guy had said something even close to that to her she'd have kneed him in the groin.

"I'm sorry. Again." She smiled apologetically, put her head back down on his shoulder and put her hand on his chest to feel his heart beating. "Tell me about going around the world."

He told her and she listened, drinking in the stories and pictures he painted of everything and everywhere she'd always dreamed of going but knew she never would. Bicycling in the south of France, hiking in Nepal, camping in Australia, banquets in Hong Kong, Nile cruises through Egypt... As he spoke, her visions of scenery and civilizations gave way to visions of Riley. Why had he dropped out of college? Why had he left the country? Was he running? Restless? In some kind of trouble?

She pushed the thoughts away. Not her concern. Riley was her fling, her fantasy, her boy toy. She shouldn't be caring about anything but their time together in the here and now.

"Sounds fabulous." She spoke lightly, stroked the hair on his chest to bring their physical relationship back to the forefront where it belonged.

"It wasn't quite as glamorous as it sounds. It was kind of a tough time, actually. I think I was…running away from my life—or rather from what my father expected of my life." Riley cleared his throat, his voice suddenly halting, unsteady, as if he were in a confessional. "Not quite the same driving force as simply wanting to experience what's out there, as you do."

Melissa nodded, and stroked down to his stomach, outlining the defined muscle with her fingertips, hardly daring to breathe. If he talked like that, shared his feelings, his vulnerable side, she was going to start caring. She didn't want to care. She wanted this to stay in the realm of fantasy adventure, where it belonged. Caring was for the guy you went to dinner with and went home to meet his parents.

She stroked the line of hair that went down his stomach and ran her hands lightly over the bulge in his pants, gratified to feel it jump and swell under the pressure of her fingers.

"Melissa…" He took her hand.

Melissa tightened her lips. Why wouldn't he let her touch him? She lifted her head and kissed his throat, slow seductive kisses up to his mouth. He responded, but cautiously, not in the passionate way he had that first night. Melissa increased the pressure, then gentled, dragged her tongue along each of his lips, sent her hand stealing down again, this time to burrow under the waistband of his pants.

A frustrated hiss of breath rushed in between his clenched teeth. The sound excited her, aroused her, gave her the permission she needed. She slid onto him and rocked against his hardness, kissing his face and neck, praying for some reaction.

She got it. He clamped her to him and flipped them so she lay underneath, pushed savagely against her, lifted to release his fly and pushed against her again through the soft heated cotton of his briefs.

Melissa swept her hands up his back and clasped him hard, savoring the solid heat of his body, meeting his thrusts, aching for the feel of him inside her, aching with a power she didn't understand, didn't want to analyze or question. She'd deliberately shattered his control so they could explore the boundaries of shared physical pleasure. That was all. That had to be all.

To her shock and horror, Riley stopped moving. Lay still, then pushed himself off her and crossed the room to stand facing away from her, muscles in his shoulders bunching as he did up his pants.

"What…what's wrong?"

He turned and faced her. "This isn't what you want, remember? You don't want plain old sex. You want *honey.*" He spat out the word as if it was an insult, then strode into Rose's kitchenette. Melissa half rose from the bed, breath coming fast, her arousal tinged with panic. "What are you doing?"

Riley emerged from the kitchen holding a plastic bottle shaped like a bear. He advanced on her and squeezed a line of honey down her belly, onto her legs and between them. "Here's your damn honey."

"Stop it." Melissa held out her hands to catch the stream, trying to shield her body from the golden liquid as if it might burn her. "You're scaring me. Stop it."

He stilled, closed his eyes and took deep breaths, drawing into himself until she could see some of the tension starting to abate. She reached and gently took the honey out of his tight fingers. What was he fighting? Why was he fighting so hard?

"Riley, are you—"

"I'm sorry, Melissa. Truly sorry. I'm finding this…difficult for some reason." He took another deep breath. "I'm sorry I scared you. I don't know what… I would never hurt you, you understand?"

Melissa nodded, her fear and shock receding. She hadn't a clue what had just happened, why he was so determined to restrain himself sexually when he obviously wanted her, but she did believe he hadn't meant to do anything more than blow off some steam. That his anger was directed at himself, not at her.

Never mind she'd just about had a heart attack in the process.

"You okay?" He met her eyes, concerned, sheepish, still tormented.

"A little shaken." She glanced at the honey. "A little sticky."

He reached out, swiped a drip of honey from her stomach and brought it to his mouth. "Sticky but sweet. You want to shower? I'll wait."

"Okay." She got up from the bed and hurried to the bathroom before she dripped honey all over Rose's Oriental rugs. Or before she dripped tears of frustration and disappointment, aware part of her still wanted him to lie on her, spread the honey around between their bodies, join with her the way men and women had been joining for millennia...so it was a damn good thing he'd nipped that in the bud by reverting to psycho-man.

The guy operated on a more intense, more passionate level than anyone she knew. Totally controlled, then savage and exciting when his control slipped. She had a feeling it didn't slip often. Something had gotten to him, shaken him up. Maybe he just wasn't used to women like her. Didn't know whether to feel paternal or sexual—the whore-versus-the-virgin thing. His usual fare was probably Xena, Warrior Princess, or women named Tawni and Bambi, with huge breasts and zero hips.

"Melissa?"

She turned, just inside the bathroom, to see him striding toward her, tall and magnificently bare chested. To her surprise, he leaned into the room and pressed a soft, lingering kiss on her mouth. "Take your time."

Melissa nodded, closed the door and slumped against it, reliving the warm pressure of his lips, feeling like she'd just been through a hyphenated hurricane. Storm, then calm, then another storm, now into new peace—but after that kiss, a peace tainted with something dangerously warm and fuzzy that was making her very nervous.

She pulled off the underwear and dumped it into the sink, showered quickly and wrapped herself in a rose-colored towel, making a mental note to take it back to her place to wash with the honey-coated lingerie.

A strange squeak sounded through the door, like wood being tortured. Melissa stood still, hand to her throat. What was he doing now?

For some reason, the ensuing silence wasn't reassuring. Instinctively, she turned on the water in the sink so he wouldn't know she was listening. Okay, so maybe she was being a tad paranoid. After all, attacking a woman with honey wasn't exactly excessive force with a deadly weapon. There must be a nice, safe, reasonable explanation for all the bizarre noises emanating from Rose's living room. Right?

Of course, there was also the escaped mental patient possibility, or the ex-con psychopath, or perhaps a graduate of the Ted Bundy School of Dating. Her instinct told her to trust Riley, but what did she know? She'd like to be able to think *other* people might be fooled, but *she* could tell when someone was warped underneath. But then so would everyone.

She whirled and marched to the door. This was ridiculous. The man had probably moved a chair and its legs had scraped on the floor. Her imagination was way out of line.

The bathroom door opened silently under her gentle push. Melissa waited a beat, then stuck her head out into the room and froze.

Riley stood in front of Rose's dresser, methodically searching through the drawers.

Melissa blinked. *Please don't let him be looking for lacy nothings to take home and try on.* Even a bestial slut from hell had her limits.

Riley turned his head as if he'd heard her thoughts. Their eyes met.

Melissa stepped into the room, feeling suddenly

very calm and in control, even naked under a bath towel that wasn't hers.

"What are you doing?"

He grinned a sly grin and held up a tiny scrap of elastic and lace. "Looking for inspiration for you. You looked fabulous in red, but I can't claim to be up on all the current styles of lingerie. Seemed like Rose might be a good research subject."

"Oh." Melissa nodded, feeling totally foolish and strangely disappointed. Obviously her thrilling trip to the dark side hadn't been dark and thrilling enough, so her imagination, fueled by Penny's nervous speculation, had added all sorts of dangerous and exciting and totally ridiculous possibilities.

The problem was that if he kept exploding all the dangerous and exciting and totally ridiculous possibilities, she was left with the strange longing she felt when he talked about his life, and the strange longing she felt those times he kissed her like he meant it.

And taking in the infinitesimal likelihood that someone like Riley would experience similar strange longings for someone like Melissa made that the most dangerous possibility of all.

7

SLATE DREW HIS PAINTBRUSH down the doorjamb, leaving a glistening trail of pristine white. Big improvement. He glanced across the porch at Rose, absorbed in touching up a window frame. Paint smudged her forehead and speckled her short hair. Her features were set in lines of intense concentration, a blessed relief from the eager smile she usually kept plastered on. Now, lost in the task, she'd relaxed her guard, become more natural.

They'd been working for two days solid, cleaning, painting, repairing. Ever since that first afternoon, when Rose had offered out of the blue to help fix up the place, and he'd looked around and suddenly seen the cottage through her eyes.

Gray, dusty, peeling, unadorned. How had he let it get to that point? Somewhere along the way, with the stress and grief and sheer time involved nursing his mom, he'd stopped paying attention.

He dipped the brush again and painted down farther, watching the sanded, graying wood refreshed to a satiny white. Rose had embraced the project—obviously something she'd welcomed to stave off the boredom of being stuck here, so far removed from her party life. She'd been a tremendous help, seeing what needed to be done, offering suggestions for further improvements, and pitching in, even when the going got messy.

Other than that, she was driving him completely crazy.

There were moments he thought he'd tapped into who she really was—tiny flashes of life, of spirit, even temper, that he'd want to grab and hold on to, extract into a whole person, shattering the careful cocoon of blandness she'd wrapped herself in.

Of course, given what he knew of her from Riley and the FBI, the insulting irony was that she probably thought she'd made herself into the kind of woman who would please him. He wiped disgustedly at a splatter of paint on the floor. As if he could possibly find a spineless female attendant irresistible.

He wrapped his brush in plastic and sauntered over to watch her work. She left that horrible wig off now, thank goodness, but still plastered on the makeup with a vengeance, as if she needed more of a mask to hide behind, and wore his mother's clothes rolled up here and tied together there to show as much of her body as possible.

He glanced at the firm bare skin around her waist. That was driving him crazy, too, but in an entirely different way. The woman was beautiful, sexy as hell and smart—when she forgot herself enough to show a brain. He went to bed frustrated every night, knowing she was sleeping in the same house, in his old bed, feminine and desirable even in threadbare flannel pajamas.

What made his frustration worse was that he could have her if he wanted. She'd been broadcasting you-can-if-you-want-to messages around the clock. But he didn't want her this way, didn't want her doctored up in some grossly misguided effort to please him. He wanted her free, natural, coming to him because she wanted him, not because she thought he wanted her.

In the meantime, he was ready to lose it.

"You missed a spot." He pointed carelessly and purposely smudged her work, trying, as he'd been trying for two days, to get a rise out of her.

"Oh, gosh, Slate. Sorry about that." She kept her face down, making him hope she was cursing him black-and-blue under her breath. "Maybe you should do the windows. You do a better job than I do."

"Yep. I really do. But then men are generally better at these things, don't you think?" He tried to keep the smile off his unshaved face, wondering if it would be too much if he scratched his belly and belched.

"Really? I didn't realize." She rose from the near-perfect job and surveyed it critically. "Doesn't look too bad, though. For a woman."

Slate raised his eyebrows. Was he imagining that bite in her tone? Well, well. He might just have managed to aggravate Ms. Rose. *Hallelujah.*

"Maybe you're tired." He made his own tone soothing, condescending, the tone used by men accustomed to blaming female hormones for their own mistakes, and had the grim satisfaction of seeing Rose flinch. "Want to take a break? Go down to the shore for a bit?"

"Sure, if you'd like to."

Slate stopped himself from shouting *Who cares what I want, what do* you *want?* as he'd been stopping himself all weekend. He nodded tightly. "Yes. I'd like to."

"Then let's go."

Out on the steps to the uneven shore path, he gestured for her to precede him, wondering if she'd try faking any more falls. She'd tried that the first day while he was showing her around. A giant dramatic spill over nothing. After he realized she was just bestowing on him the royal opportunity to have her in his arms, he'd shrugged and curtly told her to pick herself up.

Right away he'd caught his first glimpse of True Rose: surprise, a flash of hurt, anger, then the recalculations spinning through her crafty brain. He could almost imagine them. *Michael Slater, male file AB-364. Sunday, July 2. Continue subservient act at full force, but stand by for deletion of further helpless fall activity. Subject does not appear responsive.*

In front of him, Rose batted away a spruce branch and strode through the raspberry plants, not seeming to mind the thorns scraping the ridiculous patches of bare skin she insisted on preserving. Slate's instincts began broadcasting some fascinating feedback. Rose was not just a tad annoyed, she was royally p.o.'d. He quickened his pace, anxious to press his advantage, hating to torture her like this, but not seeing any other way to get to her.

And he really, really wanted to get to her.

He caught up with her at the shore. They clambered out on the rock ledge, Rose's breath coming in short pants, her color high. Could he detect a trace of wetness on her lashes?

"You scratched yourself." He pointed to her calf, where an angry red scrape had been slashed across her pale skin. "That's what you get for rolling up your pants like that. I'm surprised the mosquitoes haven't eaten you alive."

She whirled to face him, smile glued on her face

as if she didn't dare allow her lips to relax for fear of what she might say, eyes sparking rage, hands clenched into murderous fists.

She was gorgeous. He wanted her. He wanted her in a way he'd wanted very few women. Possibly none.

"Come at me, Rose." He whispered the words, raised his hands in front of him, beckoning with his fingers, unable to resist the best chance he'd had so far to get past her barrier. "Come on. Say what you want. I can take it. Tell me what I am. A pig. A jerk. Come on. Let me hear it."

She parted her lips, took in a quick rush of air as if she were about to speak. Slate waited, every muscle tense. *Come on, Rose. Come on. You're safe with me.*

For a second he thought he'd won. Thought he'd been able to push her over the edge, that she was about to abandon Suzi Spineless and let loose the verbal abuse he richly deserved.

Instead, she turned away and stared out at the ocean, gulping breaths of the spicy sea breeze, as if forcing herself to relax.

He lunged forward without thinking, grabbed her arm and turned her back around. "Don't do that. Don't disappear from me."

He watched in unbearable frustration as she shut down, as the life went out of her face and eyes, as she retreated into that bland creature he'd grown to detest.

"I'm sorry." Her voice was smooth, careful. "I don't know what you mean, Slate. You seem to have this idea that I'm hiding something from you. That I'm someone different from the woman you see every day. I'm sorry if I'm not who you want me to be, but this is who I am.''

"Bullshit." The word erupted out of him, angry and savage in the peaceful beauty of the scenery around them. "You're much more, Rose. I know it, I've seen it. I don't understand why you keep that fabulous woman locked away. I don't understand."

For a second the life flared again in her face, then faded into confusion and uncertainty before she carefully stamped it out, like a good, responsible Girl Scout on a camping trip. "I don't know what— I don't know *how* to be what you want."

"That's exactly what I mean." He took a deep breath to ease the shaking frustration in his voice, and forced himself to continue in a low, even tone. "I don't want you to be anything for me. I want you to be yourself."

"I am myself. I am always myself." She gave a little laugh, supposed to be a careless giggle, but which sounded quavery and miserable. "Who else could I be?"

He stared into her face, her blue eyes tinged with anguish under the colored layers of shadow, her too-red mouth only a few inches away, and felt crushing disappointment. How could he tell her any more plainly? He didn't want the damn Girl Scout. He wanted Rose, free and vibrant, as he'd glimpsed her agonizingly few times, as he could only imagine she could be. "Rose, you haven't been yourself for so long I think you've forgotten how."

She tightened her lips, wrapped her arms around herself. "That's a horrible thing to say to someone."

"Yes. It is. And I damn well wish it weren't true."

He dropped her arm and turned away, wanting to

throw something, sock someone, run ten miles uphill without stopping. Instead, he stared out into the bay, at the islands cloaked with pines turned yellowy-green by the sunlight. The incoming tide sloshed little waves onto the base of the ledge at his feet. Gulls squawked and wheeled out over the bay. Boat engines roared and faded into the distance. Behind him Rose was silent. Was it even remotely possible to reach her? Would she ever allow herself to listen hard enough to hear what he was saying? He couldn't bear to think of the waste—a woman like Rose going through life denying herself every honest part of it.

"Slate, what's that?"

Her cheerful tone was forced—casual conversation, tea-party chatter. He turned irritably and followed her pointing finger. A large bird flew past, showing a white head and dark body, graceful wings beating a slow, unhurried rhythm. His irritation subsided into the familiar thrill of watching the magnificent creatures. "An eagle. There's a pair nesting on Jonas Island. You can see the nest in one of the trees if you know where to look."

"Show me. Please."

He came up beside her, recognizing her peace offering for what it was, and accepting reluctantly. The war was still his to win. He leaned in close and pointed so her eyes could follow the exact path of his finger, and so he could innocently indulge his need to be near her. Her hair blew in the breeze and tickled his cheek. She smelled of paint and pine instead of that horrendously sweet perfume she'd worn the first day or so.

"Right there." He held his arm steady, straight out.

"That tree next to the nearly dead one with the green topknot."

"Oh, yes! I see it."

The eagle approached the island; a second bird rose from the trees as if in greeting. "There's Mrs. Eagle, see her?"

"Yes, yes!" Rose clapped her hands like an ecstatic child, gave in to natural ebullient laughter. "Oh, Slate, it's fabulous."

He grinned and shook his head. Two birds had accomplished in ten seconds what he'd been trying and failing to do for days. "They return to the same nest every year, keep adding on to it. Some nests can get to be six feet across."

"No kidding." Rose turned rapturous eyes on him—eyes blue and unselfconsciously joyous. He felt pulled in by them, lifted, pumped and riding a testosterone rush he hadn't experienced in years. She made him feel so damn good.

"What...else?" Her smile faltered, as if she suddenly realized he was staring at her with all his hunger out in the open. "The eagles..."

He stepped closer so he had to look nearly straight down to see her face, and put his hands on her slender, bare waist. "They mate for life. One male, one female...for their whole adult lives."

The words came out huskily and hung in the sea air between them. Rose's eyes widened; her lips parted; she started to back away.

"Slate..."

He pulled her against him and kissed her as if he'd been waiting for this kiss his entire life. The push of her hands against his chest slowly relaxed and, unbelievably, she responded, pressed herself close, wrapped her arms around his neck. He lifted her off the ground and swung her slowly around, still kissing her, giddy like a kid. So sweet. So good.

She broke off the kiss and buried her head in his shoulder, her breaths heaving almost into sobs. Slate put her down and stroked her back as if he were comforting a child, wildly triumphant. He'd done it. God bless him, he'd done it. She was his.

"You okay?" He pried her head off his shoulder, held her chin and smiled tenderly, examining her tight features, enormous eyes. His triumph wilted, along with his smile. *Damn.* He'd scared her, nearly panicked her.

She swallowed convulsively; then, to his horror, her face reverted to blankness. Her eyes half-closed, she tipped her head back and pouted like some cheesy Marilyn Monroe impersonator.

"Oh, Slate," she whispered. "Kiss me again."

He let her go abruptly, swung around and stalked back toward the path to the house. A huge cedar tilted toward the ocean at the edge of the rock; he leaned his hand on it and glanced back, registering her shock and dismay with a certain amount of satisfaction.

He wasn't going to play her gallant lover now. Not after she'd sullied what had been so good between them. *Oh, Slate. Kiss me again.* He sneered. He didn't want that woman. *Yes, Slate. No, Slate. Whatever you want, Slate.* Spending time with that version of Rose was like living with a mirror, all your wants and needs reflected, no chance of penetrating the glass to see what lay on the other side.

He strode up the path, pushing aside the overgrown grasses and raspberry plants, his body still remembering their moment of true connection. For those few seconds in his arms, Rose had been kissing him for real. Honest, clean passion had arrowed through both of them, exposing who they really were. No fakery. No role-playing.

He climbed up onto the porch and unwrapped his paintbrush, determined to get back to work as if nothing had happened between them, as if he hadn't just experienced the most powerful male-female encounter of his life. One thing Slate had in spades was patience. That glimpse into Rose, that small taste of her, had only fueled his desire to explore the rest. Sooner or later, the mirror had to crack.

ROSE TURNED OVER for the six thousandth time and buried her face in her pillow. She couldn't sleep. In Boston she'd been a champion insomniac, but here in Maine she'd slept like a rock. Now the worry machine was going full tilt.

She hadn't written to her mom this week. Not that her mom would probably notice; she didn't even recognize her daughter anymore. But the weekly letter made Rose feel she was keeping the link between them alive, in her own mind, anyway. This week she hadn't written.

Then there was Melissa. Was she okay? Had she and Tom hit it off? Were they still meeting at her apartment or had they moved to Melissa's place, where they'd be safer?

Was the van still parked in front of her apartment? Was Senator Mason in some kind of trouble? Had whoever hired Gel Man and Broken Nose roughed them up for losing her trail? Had the two thugs given up? Were they still looking? Would they find her?

Rose clenched her fist on the pillow. It was no use.

She was worrying as hard as possible about everything she could think of, avoiding the one thing that was really bothering her.

Slate.

He was the most complicated, most confusing man she'd ever met. He didn't respond to anything the way she expected, the way he was supposed to. The very first day she'd tripped over a log half-buried under leaves and moss, and had looked to him for help, figuring he'd love the chance to rush in for the rescue. Rescue was obviously his thing. Look how he'd opened his house to a stranger, a woman in need. For all he knew, he was risking his life to protect her.

But no. He'd snapped at her to get up, seemed annoyed she'd looked to him in the first place. Okay. Maybe she'd gotten him wrong. So she'd tried another tack, asserted herself, suggested they fix up the dreary house. He'd looked around in shock, as if her boldness appalled him, as if she'd better keep her mouth shut in the future. Then he'd taken charge of the renovation work, barking commands, criticizing her work....

Sometimes it felt as if he was goading her, deliberately trying to make her lose her temper. Some men were into power issues, trying to make themselves appear more in control by making those around them lose theirs. But Slate didn't quite fit that mold, either; she didn't sense he was enjoying trying to make her crazy.

So what was with this man? He had her completely off balance from the moment she got up in the morning until she fell into bed at night, confused and exhausted. Rose wasn't used to being off balance. Not around men. Men were her specialty, her area of expertise. She'd never met one she couldn't get along with, one who didn't, at the very least, respond to overtures of friendship.

Rose couldn't figure out Slate at all. And in the midst of this bewildering, draining attempt to make their stay together pleasant, she had begun to crack, show temper, show strain. She hadn't done that since the seventh grade, when Roger Doldens had called her mom a slut. Rose had blackened his eye and borne the brunt of the blame at school and at home. Since then, losing control had become foreign to her.

Rose thrashed over onto her back and stared up into the darkness. But that wasn't the worst of it. The worst of it was that she had started to want him. Not in her usual fun, affectionate way. Not in her patented take-it-or-leave-it, oh-what-the-hell kind of way. She wanted him. In a hot, wild, desperate way she'd never felt before.

And it scared the bejeezus out of her.

Wanting something that much meant either you got it and were ever after afraid of losing it, or you didn't get it, and you hurt forever. She'd never ever wanted to want anyone or anything this much.

When he'd kissed her today, she'd gotten one forbidden taste of what it could be like to be with him. In a word: *heaven.* Then the desire had wound around inside her, slithered and swelled and threatened to squeeze the life out of her, and she'd had to fight. Fight for it to uncoil, release her, so she could escape back to the refuge of not feeling, of simply being. Find a way he could still have the kisses he wanted from her, but without risking, without hurting.

Immediately, he'd rejected her. As if she disgusted

him. As if he'd been caught kissing beauty and she'd turned into the beast right under his lips.

He knew. He was so tuned in to her feelings, so powerfully perceptive, so much deeper than the men she knew, in empathy, in sensitivity, that he could sense exactly who Rose was, and the exact moment she'd tried to deny him.

On the rocks today he'd gotten closer to the truth of her than anyone ever had. For the past ten years not one man had ever questioned who she was, whether she was more than she appeared. Not one had ever looked past the positive glow she spun onto him, and tried to find her own inner light.

God, he frightened her.

A tear squeezed out from under her tightly closed lids. She dashed it away with her fist and took a savage breath to brace herself back into control.

An owl whoo-whooed out in the darkness; some animal rustled nearby in a probably terrified response. Rose shuddered, filled with sudden longing for the safety of crowds and electric lights and 9-1-1. In spite of how much she'd come to love the Maine coast, in spite of how she'd discovered unexpected homesickness for the rural Midwestern country of her childhood, this place was creepy as hell at night, especially when she still felt hunted. Too quiet; every little noise jumped out. Too deserted; no one could hear if she screamed.

A stick cracked out in the woods near the house. Rose started, her nerves by now shredded. Another crack. Then a rustle. Something moving through the woods. Something big.

Her breathing flew up into her chest. Had they

found her? Even here? Were they standing outside, waiting to burst in and start shooting?

Silence.

Then the regular snap and rustle of steps, but nearer now. Panic swelled. Rose tried to pull in a calming breath, but it stuttered uselessly into her lungs. *Get me out of here.* She jumped from the bed and rushed to the door, then stopped, body trembling, leaning her hands against the cool wood.

She wasn't going up to Slate now. Not shaky and scared and damn-it-all-to-hell vulnerable. She'd want him to take her in his arms, tell her everything would be fine. He'd probably hand her a gun and tell her to go outside and shoot whatever it was herself.

She grabbed a flashlight and crept to the window, holding her breath, trembling uncontrollably. *Please, please...* Chances were in wilderness like this the noises were animal, not human. Right?

Rose lifted the shade a crack and looked out. Moonlight spilled onto the birch trunks, illuminated them to a ghostly glowing white, created stark shadows on the ground.

Movement. Near the house. She swallowed her panic and lifted the light, then burst into a breathless, relieved chuckle. Not human. Porcupine.

She slumped against the sill until her relief-weakened body wanted to move again. *Okay, Rose. Okay.* She turned back into the room, took one step toward her bed and stopped. The tears came. Not gently and beautifully as they did in Boston, but big ugly tears and wracking sobs that sounded like someone choking, being violently sick.

She dove onto the bed and buried her face in the

pillow. What were the odds she could hide a half hour of this from Slate in a tiny, uninsulated cabin?

None. She could hear his steps coming down the stairs, the sharp creak and crack of the pine. She put her hand over her mouth, tried to stop her body shaking.

He knocked at the door. "Rose, what's going on?"

She shook her head, unable to speak, unable to move. The door opened. She heard his exclamation, felt his weight on the bed, his body above her, his arms around her, her name whispered.

She gave in to her need, sat up and burrowed against him, relaxed into the tears.

"It's okay. You're okay." He whispered the words over and over, enveloping her with his strength, stroking her back with warm, calming hands. "It's okay. You're safe with me."

She nodded into his chest, pressing closer, absorbing his scent and his hard male comfort. It would be okay. She was okay. She was safe.

As long as he never let go.

8

RILEY FINISHED THE COAT of spar urethane protecting the warm, reddish-brown stain on Leo's dresser and stepped back to look. Nice piece. Beautiful symmetry, clean lines.

He pictured Leo taking out clothes for his skinny little body and frowned. Something wasn't quite right. The dresser was beautiful: elegant design, flawless workmanship. But Leo was six years old. Imagined next to his nephew's helter-skelter energy, the piece suddenly looked rigid, stern...and a little too adult.

So what, then? What would make it more suitable, more...whimsical maybe, for a six-year-old?

Riley glared at the dresser. How the hell would he know? His brain did logic and intuition, cunning and deceit. He didn't do whimsical. Leo would forgive him, of course, but Riley wanted to do this right. He adored his nephew, loved the time they spent together, but always sensed uneasily that Leo was carefully on his best behavior. The way Riley had been when his overly venerable uncle Norman took him anywhere as a kid. This dresser would only reinforce Leo's impression, reinforce the boy-man contrast when Riley desperately wanted to break it down.

Damned if he knew how to fix either the dresser or their relationship, but damned if he'd give up trying. The kid needed a man. And Riley probably needed him.

He crossed his arms and stared at the dresser. What? Colorful paint? Stencils? Stickers? Maybe he should ask his sister. Except she was distracted, worried about Leo, who hadn't been feeling well. How she managed being a single parent, he hadn't a clue.

A picture of Melissa shot into his mind, as pictures of her had been doing regularly since he met her. Laughing and rolling her eyes when her weird fascination with ice didn't turn out to be quite what she'd hoped. Melissa would know, too. She'd probably be able to suggest thirty things off the top of her head—how to fix the dresser *and* the outings with his nephew. She had this incredible directness about her; she seemed so tapped into life, to joy, to energy. Next to her he felt like…a dresser. Rigid, stern and a little too adult.

His shop phone rang. He gave one last scowl at the dresser and picked it up.

"What's taking so damn long, Riley?"

Riley rolled his eyes. Captain Watson didn't even bother identifying himself. "Excuse me?"

"Her apartment is the size of a closet, for crissake. I've got other cases to spend time on. I can't wait all month for this."

Riley wrestled back a surge of anger before it found its way into his voice, noting the underlying panic in Watson's usually confident nasal tone. "If it's there, I'll find it."

"It's got to be there. This Rose chick still hasn't given anything away? Hasn't told you anything?"

"No." Riley gave a small, satisfied smile. As he suspected, the captain didn't know Rose had disappeared. "Rose doesn't know what she has. I'm sure of it."

Watson swore obscenely. "Fat lot of good that does us. The chief is ready to fry my balls in lard."

Riley raised an eyebrow. Since when did someone as cocky as Watson admit to worrying over the chief's displeasure? "Having to be in the apartment with her there makes this a slow job. You want it done faster? Get a warrant and send your guys in. Rip the place apart."

"And risk whoever's turned traitor getting his hands on it? That portrait would be out of our jurisdiction in a heartbeat. Just get the damn job done." Watson slammed down the phone.

Interesting. Riley immediately dialed Ted Barker's number.

"Ted Barker, FBI."

Riley's lips twitched. The guy probably had FBI tattooed on his privates.

"Riley Anderson. Watson just called me, sounding a little too antsy about finding the portrait."

"Really."

Something about the way Ted Barker, FBI, said the word made it sound as if he wasn't entirely surprised. Riley's instincts kicked in big time. Something stank around Charles Watson, and the Feds could smell it.

"We want you to stop searching, Anderson."

Riley tensed. "Why?"

"We're closing in on the police link to Allston. We believe he's hanging back right now, waiting for you to find the portrait for him. If you stop looking, someone will get nervous enough to make a mistake."

Riley clenched the phone to his ear. That meant—

"So you won't need to go on any more...dates."
Ted Barker, FBI, coughed politely. The man had
probably never been laid in his life. "We'll be in
touch if we need you further."

Riley hung up the phone, muscles resisting his
commands as if they wanted to move in slow motion.
So that was it. Dismissed. His part in the operation
was over. Not surprising. He was more surprised the
Feds had let him and Slate share their territory even
for the few days they had. Probably to keep Watson
happy while they checked him out. If Watson was the
leak to Allston, he'd have needed Riley to get the
portrait to him before the cops and/or Feds got hold
of it legally and kept it away from Allston. Now the
Feds would sit back and wait for their pale-eyed
mouse with the thinning hair and penchant for grease
to blunder in their maze. With Allston undoubtedly
leaning hard, undoubtedly wishing he'd never bribed
Senator Mason with the portrait in the first place,
Watson was starting to sound desperate enough to do
just that.

So. Riley had done his part. Melissa might be disappointed to miss the rest of her adventure, but they'd
had fun. Maybe she'd learned enough about what she
was after so she wouldn't mind. Maybe she'd find
someone else. Riley could easily come up with some
plausible excuse for discontinuing their affair. That
was his job. He could go back to his other cases now.
Move along. Clear his mind.

Refocus. He took his brushes over to his workbench
and jabbed them into a jar of paint thinner. Truth to
tell, he was a little relieved not to have to deceive her
anymore. Melissa had been getting pretty insistent
about wanting him to climax during their trysts. He

didn't like the idea of mixing business with sex. Would have felt somehow he'd crossed the line into taking advantage of his position if he allowed himself more pleasure than he already took seeing her sexuality blossom under his fingers. Now he wouldn't have to fight that battle.

He held up a brush to check the bristles and noticed it shaking. Strange. He picked up another in his other hand. Same thing. Riley took a deep breath, knowing what was coming, and waited for the denied emotion to hit him, like the idiot surfing in a hurricane waits in stunned acceptance for the tidal wave to overtake him.

Damn. The brushes landed back in the jar of paint thinner with tuneful plops. Riley backed up until he felt the wall behind him, then slid down to a squat, laced his fingers and bent his head. He was full of it. Way, way full of it.

He wanted her. He still wanted her. He wanted her more than ever because now he had no convenient reason to see her. Because one call from Ted Never-Gets-Laid Barker had ripped away the pretense, the pathetic sheltering excuse he hid behind, and exposed his need. He wanted her. Not just her body. Her. To talk to, to touch, to laugh with. He didn't care if they got naked or not.

Their date the night before had been a near total catastrophe. From his sudden nightmarish need to unburden himself about his past, which she understandably wanted no part of, to the horrendous moment when he realized all he wanted to do was hold her tight, to make love to her the slow, tender, simple way, to protect her from any and all men who might hurt her if she continued this sexual charade. All that to the near disastrous ending, when his emotion made him careless and she'd caught him going through Rose's things.

Riley shut his eyes, remembering his horror, the massive energy required to hide it, the fear that he'd blown his cover. And the creeping, deep-down suspicion that he feared breaking their twisted, tenuous association even more. His feelings for her were becoming a hell of a lot more than professional.

Melissa only wanted sex. To experiment with him as if he were unidentified matter in a petri dish. He gave a bitter laugh. Too bad Slate wasn't here to slap sense into him, and stop him from behaving like a combination outraged virgin and puppy-love schoolboy.

Regroup. Reexamine. Turn the same facts around another way and reinterpret them. He got up from his crouch and mounted the stairs, from the airless basement into the breezy light of his first floor. He still didn't believe a woman like Melissa could be happy with sex for the sake of sex. Maybe he could ride that part out, give her the fling she wanted, then prove it to her. Surrender to this crazy longing and make love to her the way he wanted. Show her what should really be between a man and a woman, give her more pleasure than all the kinky devices in the world.

Make a plan. What would outraged-virgin-schoolboys do in this situation? Riley smiled and shook his head. If he had to ask, it had been way too long.

Melissa might freak, might balk, might squirm and think of excuses, but you never knew. She might also smile that dynamite shy smile that turned his insides loopy, and say yes.

Either way, at their next meeting, in the middle of whatever kinky creations they could cook up, Riley Anderson was going to ask Melissa Rogers out on a good, old-fashioned date.

MELISSA SIGHED as the last sparkling explosion of firework stars faded from the night sky over the Charles River. The crowd around her cheered and stood, packing away picnics and blankets before attempting to make its way home, a huge flowing river of people being absorbed back into the dark city. She smiled at her friends from her alma mater, Boston University, and said goodbye, not in the mood to linger. Brad, a blond preppy guy she'd always secretly lusted after, shot to his feet, put his arms around her and tried to persuade her to stay. She brushed him off, laughing, and waved good-night. Even his unusual attentiveness tonight didn't do much to make her feel part of the celebration, though it didn't hurt.

She generally loved being in the middle of this mass of humanity on the Fourth of July, humanity united by love of partying, if not of country. But for some reason this year she'd been strangely lonely, dogged by thoughts and questions about Riley— whether and how he was celebrating, whether and how he was thinking of her...

Melissa rolled her eyes. As if. Just because Riley was the embodiment of her every fantasy didn't mean she was remotely the same for him.

This preoccupation wasn't at all part of her bargain with the dark side. Not at all what she wanted to be feeling. Instead of being thrilled with the fabulous physical experiences, all she could think about was his intensity, that sense of restrained power that made her feel protected and endangered at the same time. The delightful sense of satisfaction, of triumph when she made him smile or laugh. Admiration for the fact that he'd had the guts to drop out of his preprogrammed life and tour around the world, that he'd grabbed the chance to become so richly colored by experience, where she stopped short every time.

Face it, the experiment was turning out to be a disaster. She was a failure as a sex goddess. Had she really thought she had even a third of the female power Rose had? That she could use a man's body and toss him aside in the interim, indulge her physical needs and leave her emotions untouched?

All Riley had to do was touch her, put his hands on her body, and she went nuts wanting him to—

"Now I know what cattle feel like at roundup time."

Melissa glanced up and met the frankly interested hazel eyes of a nice-looking, brown-haired, thirty-something guy shuffling next to her in the enormous crush of people. He winked and grinned a dynamite grin. "Want to wait out the crowds? We have a place staked out over there."

He pointed to a blanket well-stocked with attractive Yuppie types, mostly male. Melissa blinked, then smiled politely, shook her head and thanked him anyway. He shrugged and disappeared into the crowd, leaving her slightly stunned. Did that just happen? That never happened. He was seriously cute, and looked to be just her type. If not for her strange solitary mood, she would have been tempted—once she got over the shock.

The crowd thinned slightly and she joined the throng headed for the Charles Station T-Stop, unable to suppress a lingering smile. A male friend had once told her women could *tell* when he'd been getting good sex. They flocked to him. He'd sworn they could smell it on him.

Well, that idea was pretty disgusting, but Melissa couldn't help remembering the concept now. First Brad, then this guy…

Okay, maybe she wasn't a *total* failure as a sex goddess.

Half an hour later, she managed to cram onto a Red Line train, and swayed and bumped her way to the Harvard Square stop. She came up the steps, out into the square, and nearly bumped into the major hunk who lived on the floor below her, who she'd managed to smile at in the elevator a few times when she was feeling particularly brave.

He greeted her and fell into step beside her; they chatted easily up Mass. Ave to Garden Street, past the Cambridge Common into their building and into the elevator. At his floor he turned abruptly and opened his mouth to say something, then appeared to change his mind, turned beet-red and fled with a mumbled good-night.

Melissa stared at the doors closing slowly behind him. *Ho-ly mo-ly.* He'd been about to ask her out. He *blushed*, for heaven's sake. A man she could barely summon up the nerve to glance at. *What was up?*

The elevator reached her floor; she strode out and flung herself into her apartment, totally hyped. Maybe her self-condemnation had been a little premature. Maybe her adventure with Riley *had* changed her. Maybe she wasn't quite the disaster as a bestial slut from hell she feared.

She prowled around her apartment, trying to find

an appropriate outlet for her pent-up energy, and finally decided to watch the *Sex and the City* tapes a
friend had lent her.

An hour and a half and an endless parade of differently partnered couples later, she rewound the tape
and pressed the eject button with a flourish. *Ha!* That
was it. The life she was heading for. This affair with
Riley would be the opening of the floodgates that
would lead her to a tidal wave of sexual satisfaction.

The tape ejected from the machine with a groaning
whine of motor and gears. Melissa slid it back into
its case and went into the bathroom to brush her teeth,
brimming with new confidence. She'd see Riley tomorrow night. After the hit-and-miss ride of last Saturday, she'd make sure they could settle into a more
comfortable flow this time. Skip the emotional tug of
war that unearthed feelings she didn't want to have.
Get into and onto and around the bed and do whatever
felt right.

She grimaced at herself in the bathroom mirror,
toothpaste dripping out of one corner of her mouth.
Except that last Saturday night what had felt so right
was wanting him to make love to her with everything
in him instead of staying off to the side, a clothed,
casual spectator. She wanted him with her, on top of
her, inside her...

So? That was a natural human instinct. Someday
she'd indulge those deeper feelings with the guy she'd
wake up next to until death did them part. Someone
more like her—gentler, more...ordinary. Not someone who could emerge from a phone booth in a blue-
red-and-yellow costume and not make her blink. Not
someone who challenged every sense to the straining

point when she was around him. Someone who would find her as fascinating as she found him.

That said, she would like Riley to…participate more. He resisted, held back, as if he were impotent or asexual, which, judging by the width and breadth of his pants after she'd been writhing around in ecstasy in front of him for a while, was definitely not the case.

So why did he force himself to remain so irritatingly neutral? Was he neurotically modest? A voyeur? Diseased? Hideously deformed?

She snorted at the idea and nearly got toothpaste up her nose. Then laid down her brush and stared at her reflection, white foam ringing her lips. Or was he afraid of the same thing she was? That connection, that longing that had pulled them to each other, that had made them wrap themselves around each other and strive to join. Was that why he pulled away and got hostile with Mr. Honey Bear?

Melissa shook her head and spat viciously into the sink. Right. And tomorrow she'd open her front door to find Mel Gibson and Harrison Ford duking it out for her favors. Maybe he just forgot condoms. Maybe he was married. Maybe penetration went against his religion or his mommy had told him never never never do that naughty naughty thing.

Maybe he was just doing what Melissa had *asked* him to, from the beginning—staying away from the same old missionary grind.

She dragged a cream-colored towel across her mouth, stalked across the gray carpet into her bedroom and tugged on a T-shirt. Whatever the case, it didn't concern her. She was getting what she wanted from him. As long as she remained as selfish as possible, took what she needed from their relationship and concentrated on the pleasure, the affair would stay in control, stay exactly where it was supposed to.

The only change she wanted, one she might insist on tomorrow with her sex goddess status firmly reinstated, was that Riley take his own pleasure, teach her to give him release in as many ways as he wanted to give it to her.

Her toe bumped against a box under her bed as she climbed in between the plain cotton sheets. Melissa grabbed it, opened it and grinned down at the sheriff's badge and handcuffs. Would she ever have the nerve to ask Riley to use them on her?

She held them up; the light from her bedside lamp sparked off the shiny twisting metal. The fantasies of Riley shackling her to the bed or locking her wrists to the towel rack in the shower were suddenly replaced by another quite different scene. An inspiration.

Melissa's grin turned wicked. She was suddenly quite sure she'd have the nerve to use them.

Riley wasn't going to know what hit him.

9

SLATE STRETCHED HIS LEGS on the chaise and lifted his cup of coffee for a slow, warming sip. After a couple of days of thick gray fog, the sunshine and view had returned, to make one of the clear sparkling mornings for which Maine was, in his experience, unparalleled. He leaned forward on the porch to peek out the side screen, toward the east. This was his favorite time of morning, when the sun had risen on the other side of the peninsula, but hadn't yet cleared the tall pines to shine directly here. In the early light the lobster buoys glowed cheerily, like gaudy jewels scattered on the still water. Above them the sky warmed from pink to pale to blue at the horizon. Lobster boats buzzed from buoy to buoy like bees among flowers, leaving the water behind them plowed to a wavy froth.

He heard Rose up, moving around the cabin, and tried to still the tenacious, ever-optimistic hope that she'd appear in the doorway naturally rumpled and still sleepy, just out of bed wearing the ratty nightgown he'd supplied.

"Good morning."

He nodded and made himself smile, taking in her neat outfit, purchased on a cabin-fever trip into town the day before. Short stylish pants that followed the contours of her legs to midcalf, a low-necked top and a cotton sweater. As usual, she'd plastered gunk all over her face, though if he wasn't imagining it, maybe with a lighter hand today. He turned back to his coffee. Anything put on heavily enough to obscure the wholesome, beautiful lines of her features was too much for his taste.

"Looks like whoever stole the view decided to return it." Rose gestured out at the far side of the bay. "I never understood the term pea-souper until three days ago."

"The Maine coast is famous for lobster and the thickest, most tenacious fog in the country." He swung his legs over the side of the chaise and stood. "I'll get you some coffee."

"Thanks." She smiled up at him as he passed.

He went into the kitchen, poured coffee and cut her a slice of the coffeecake they'd bought at the supermarket bakery. At least he and Rose had settled into a predictable if uneasy rhythm, ever since the night he'd gone downstairs and found her in tears. He'd held her soft body against him for over an hour in the darkness of her bedroom, battling desire and the equally powerful need to help her. To release her from the burden of hiding herself and offer her...

Slate shook his head. That's where he stopped every time. Offer her what? Completion? Wholeness? The beauty of self-actualization? Did he think he was suddenly the expert of New Age psychiatry? Wanting to break a person wide-open, when neither he nor she might be able to deal with what came pouring out?

Then what?

He wasn't committed to her, hadn't promised to love, honor and cherish. This wasn't a case where "for worse" had won out over "for better." In some ways he was being selfish, wanting her to give up a defense system that worked for her, when he wasn't sure what protection he could promise in return. Except the chance to explore what might be between them. And who really knew what that was?

He brought her breakfast out onto the porch and handed it to her with a carefully friendly grin. But damn it, he ached to see her run free. See her spiritually, emotionally and yes-please-ma'am physically naked. See if they'd be as good together as he thought they could be.

She ate; he chatted amicably until she stood and took her plate into the kitchen. He followed like a smitten puppy, wondering if he could stand letting her go back to her life unchanged. Wondering if he could go back to his own life and think about her, day after day, and the parade of men she'd alter herself to please.

"The house looks really nice. A whole different place from when we arrived." Rose put her dishes in the sink and ran water into a plastic basin.

Slate nodded and glanced around. Cleaned, scrubbed, painted, polished, the house had regained the cheerful freshness his mom always maintained there. For some reason, instead of restoring comforting familiarity, the house's transition bothered him. It felt artificial, contrived, almost disrespectful, as if with the passing of his mom the house she and his dad had loved so much should be allowed to go with her. Illogical, maybe, but he couldn't shake the feeling the sprucing had negated her death, somehow.

"Slate..." Rose spoke from the sink, her back to him as she rinsed out her mug. Something in her tone made him step closer and focus attention on her profile. "Your mom must have had more things around the place."

"Things?" He tensed, suspecting what she was going to say.

"Decorations. Like, I don't know, ceramic figures or pictures you drew or things you all collected on the beach, pottery, vases—something." She put her dishes in the drying rack, turned and gestured behind him. "All those shelves. They must have had something on them. The house looks so…unlived in."

Slate crossed his arms over his chest. "She packed everything away before we left. To protect it from dust, mice, prowlers. Whatever."

He turned to go back onto the porch, movements stiff, hoping Rose would drop it.

"Why don't we dig out some things and put them around? It would look really nice. We put this much work into the house, it would be fun to cheer it up some more."

Slate stopped in the doorway to the porch, muscles rigid. All his mom's precious bits and pieces, carefully unpacked every year and set in their appointed spaces, carefully repacked and hidden before they left each September. The house's history, the family's history, now down to just him. All the years of his life, represented by carved wood and pottery and beeswax and feathers and who knew what else, in those damn boxes.

He didn't want to unpack the stuff. He didn't want to be reminded of how the house had looked when his mom was alive. She was gone and buried. Why dig her up and pretend everything was the same?

"No point. We'll only be here another week."

"Slate." Rose came up close behind him, laid her

hand on his arm. The warmth of her fingers seeped through the thick flannel of his shirt; he had to force himself not to pull away from her sympathy. "My mom has Alzheimer's. She doesn't know who I am anymore. But I write to her every week, a long letter for the nurse to read to her. I think I'll probably keep writing to her even after she dies. It...keeps her alive to me."

Her words came out low and halting, unlike her usual musical delivery. Part of Slate responded, wanting to encourage her. In that short moment she'd told him more about her life than she had the entire week they'd been here. But he couldn't. Not on this topic. He swung around. "I'm sorry about your mom. I'm glad that works for you."

"Try it." She gazed at him earnestly. "You'll be amazed how seeing things that belonged to her can bring her closer."

He shook his head, the hateful bite of grief sharp inside him. "I don't need reminders. I don't want reminders. I think that's understandable."

Rose opened her mouth to protest, then bowed her head and readjusted her features, hands clenched tightly at her side. "Yes. Okay. I'm sorry."

He took her shoulders, his own pain forgotten in the need to release hers. "You're not sorry. You don't agree. Say it, Rose. I dare you."

"It's not my place. You were right."

He gripped her hard, as if he could squeeze the confession out of her. "You think I'm wrong. You think I'm full of it. Say it."

"No." The word was abrupt and furious.

"Damn it, Rose, *say it.*"

She lifted her head, eyes freed from their shutters,

blazing rage and passion. "Okay. Fine. You want me to tell you what I think? I think you buried the woman, but you won't let her die. You think if you ignore her long enough she'll come back? Maybe you even feel guilty, that somehow you should have been able to cure her where every medical specialist couldn't, because you're so damn perfect and capable in everything you do."

He let his hands drop from her shoulders. Her words were like rasps drawn along existing wounds, scraping open grief and guilt he thought he'd already worked through.

She jabbed her thumb to her chest. "I refuse to cheat myself out of more of my mom than fate already has. Someday when you start having trouble remembering what she looked like, what she sounded like, how she smelled, you'll be standing here in this nice vacuum you've created, wondering why you ever thought locking your mom out was going to keep her in your heart forever."

Slate stared at her, stupid, unable to speak, half in awe of her power—more than he'd dreamed of—half in an agony of bewildering fear.

Rose moved forward and shoved furiously at his chest; he stepped back heavily.

"You see?" She waved her arm in a frantic arc, breath heaving in dry sobs. "This is what you wanted so much. This anger, and all this hurting between us. You think this is better?"

He nodded slowly, pulling himself out of his strange despair. "Yes. I think it's better."

"Well I *hate* it. It's ugly and painful."

He leaned toward her, willing her to accept and understand. "Because it's *real*. This is what life feels like sometimes, Rose. You talk about not cheating yourself out of your mother, while all along you're cheating yourself out of you."

She drew in a sharp breath, then burst into bitter laughter; her expression changed to one of contempt that would have chilled him except for the anguished confusion behind it.

"I don't need to learn what my life feels like from you, Michael Slater. You're not my Master, I'm not your 'Little Grasshopper.' You're just another man. And frankly, I am *sick* to *death* of men." She turned, wrenched open the door and disappeared out into the woods, bounding between the trees like a frightened deer.

Slate lunged to the door, then stopped, hands spread against the jamb, watching her disappear. He'd gone too far. Pushed her beyond anywhere he had a right to push her. If he followed right now he'd lose her.

He turned back into the house, feeling like middle age had gotten a jump start on his thirty-three years. Rose had to do this alone. Make a decision out there in the woods and come back, either open and free or shut away from him permanently.

All he had to do—all he *could* do, damn it—was wait.

ROSE SPRINTED DOWN the long-unused road in the woods behind Slate's house, pushing her body to its limit. Her feet pounded on the hard pebbled tracks or sank into patches of moss. Cobwebs collected on her face, stuck by invisible threads that resisted her clawing attempts to remove them. She couldn't stop. Her lungs protested, muscles ached, breath came in raspy gasps. Her foot twisted on an exposed root; pain shot through her ankle. *Don't stop. Can't stop.* She hopped a few steps until the pain eased and she could run on.

To the left. A path to the shore. Rose veered off and followed it, slowing to push past overgrown, scratchy spruces, her panting half sobs absorbed into the indifference of the forest. She burst into a tiny clearing, thick with sprouting alders, blackberries and cheerful red bunchberries nestling up to fallen trees.

She ran on toward the shore. She needed to escape the confinement of the woods and the cabin and Slate's demands; needed to embrace the wide-open vista of the sea.

He wanted too much from her. Too much. She scrambled down a steep eroding bank, sending an avalanche of dirt and pebbles down around her. He wanted everything, promised nothing. Thought he could pry her open like an old tin can to see if what he found inside was worth the trouble. She stumbled over the unstable rocks to the edge of the water and stood looking out, heaving air into her lungs, fighting the tears that would show weakness she didn't want even the gulls and the waves to see.

He was driving her crazy. Crazy with anger, crazy with longing. She was crazy tempted by everything about him. His eyes, his body, his gentleness, his quiet determination to get from her what he thought was best. He was the most seductive man she'd ever known, because everything about him shouted safety, trust, integrity. A guy you brought home to Mom and then stayed up all night with, doing things Mom never dreamed of.

Even from the depth of his own hurt and grief—grief for his mother, hurt Rose had inflicted—he'd pulled himself out to encourage her, to put her ahead of himself, to fight for who he believed she was.

Why wouldn't he leave her alone?

Tears came in a horrible blinding rush, contorted her mouth into a mask-of-tragedy grimace. What if she couldn't be what he wanted? What if what he saw in her wasn't even there?

"Why won't he leave me alone?" She cried the words out into the bay. A flock of cormorants bobbing in the water lifted off in panic. Her sobs mixed with hysterical laughter. God, what a picture she must make. Dusty and dirty, running nose, dripping makeup, not sure if she was laughing or crying...

The son of a bitch. He did this to her. Shattered her calm, her composure, her control. The first man who ever could. The son of a bitch.

On impulse she picked up a small rock, hurled it into the water and watched it land with a satisfying splash. Son of a bitch. She picked up another, and another larger one, hurled them farther, faster, kept up a steady stream until she was laughing, panting, swearing, calling him every name she could think of. Splash after splash until her arms ached, her hands and forearms bled from barnacle scratches, and sweat joined the dust and tears to stain her face.

Finally a rock so big she could barely lift it. She tottered to a nearby ledge, stumbled, nearly slipped, hoisted it, muscles straining, bellowed out a war cry and let it fall with a *tch-thunk* that pulled all her anger down with it. Swallowed into the green icy water in a fizzy rush of bubbles.

She backed up shakily, caught her foot on a rock and sat down hard. A far-off gull indulged in wild maniacal squawking. The ocean smoothed over after

her assault on its surface. Cormorants returned and
settled huffily back into place. The breeze stilled to
an occasional whisper.

The son of a bitch. She was crazy about him.

A lone bird soared across the sky, heading toward
its nest on Jonas island. Rose shaded her eyes and
peered out to watch it, no more than a flapping black
blob above the horizon. *They mate for life. One male,
one female...for their whole adult lives.*

Rose let her head fall back, managed a long, calming breath. Falling in love was supposed to be that
simple. Full of natural joy and blushing acceptance.
Not this twisted agony of fear and mistrust.

She stood, muscles in her legs and arms trembling,
and picked her way carefully back to the bank, scrambled up, loosening more dirt to add to the layer already on her clothes and skin. She pushed her way
through the trees, back to the road, and trudged on in
the same direction she'd been running in. Sooner or
later she'd go back and face him. But not now, not
yet. Not until she managed to make sense of all the
emotions, all the factors, all the risks.

Another path led off the road up a small mossy
hill, up to his family's well. She followed it slowly,
grunting as she struggled up a ledge, her body as
beaten and weary as her mind. Somewhere along this
path was an old hand pump, still hooked up, but
hardly used since gasoline motors had replaced it.
Slate's parents had left the old-fashioned version in
place for emergencies and sentimental reasons.

One more scramble up, around a cluster of birches,
and the pump came into view in a small clearing,
freshly painted black, mounted on a gray wooden
platform as if it were a shrine. Rose stepped up care-

fully and caught hold of the handle. Up. Down. The metal screeched in protest, but resistance told her water would come soon. Up. Down. She slapped at a mosquito, then another, attracted by her sweat and heat. Up. Down. Up. Down. Then a clear stream of water. She put a hand under it and laughed out loud. Cold. Clear. From the earth.

Up. Down. She filled her hand, splashed it up on her face. Up. Down. Up. Down. The stream was stronger now, more constant. She put her whole head under, scrubbed at her face with her free hand, gasping at the icy cold, and laughed again.

Water dripped down into the collar of her shirt. She stood and stared at the pump. Her head felt clean and cool, her body stained and hot.

The urge came on her quick and frantic; her fingers flew to the buttons of her sweater. She tore it off, kicked it away, feverishly unbuttoned her shirt and flung it to rest on the grass and moss. Unhooked her bra, sent it spinning; shed the rest of her clothes and took hold of the pump handle again.

The cold water took her breath away. She gasped and shivered, gave a little scream and ducked under again, rubbing her body to take away the sweat and dirt, the blood from her arms. Then stood under the water and let it flow over her shoulders, her breasts, her back, her legs until she felt clean and light and glowing from the cold.

She rinsed her clothes next, laid them to dry on a rock in the strong sunshine, and stretched out beside them on the moss. The clear air warmed her, dried her, caressed her. She let herself think again of Slate. *One male, one female...for their whole adult lives.* What was it about him that made that sound so noble, so idyllic, so tempting? Was it just the spell of this amazing place? The spell of that amazing man that made her life in Boston—her cherished, man-littered life—seem so inadequate, so artificial?

One male. One female. Was that what he wanted from her? Could she risk finding out if she could give him that much? What if, after all this, she wasn't what he wanted at all? Stripped of her makeup, her charms, her mystery…what was left? After you gave yourself to someone so completely, what the hell was left?

The sun beat down on her skin, warmed her, made her feel alive and whole and safe here in the woods. She thought again of Slate, how he'd held her that night in her bed, as if she were his precious child. How he'd kissed her, standing down on the rocks, as if she were his ultimate fantasy of woman. How he'd looked to her with pleading eyes that morning, as if she could fix everything wrong in his world if she'd only try.

She lay there as her clothes dried and the morning turned into afternoon, then finally sat up, stood, feeling clean and clear and slightly sunburned. Clean and clear as the sweet air around her, cleaner and clearer than she'd ever felt in her life.

And she decided. Stood up, got dressed in her still-damp, wrinkly clothes with hands that shook, and walked back through the sunlit trees and leaf-strewn boulders to the house where she knew he waited.

SLATE EMERGED from the shower for the second time in four hours, towel wrapped around his hips, muscles protesting every movement. He'd spent the morning clearing brush, cutting down dead trees, digging out alders and chopping firewood at a frenzied, vengeful pace, one eye always to the woods, to the path, watching for Rose. Then he'd stopped, showered, eaten a few bites of what was supposed to be lunch, sat on the porch for a good six or seven seconds, picked up the chainsaw again and worked himself until he was coated once more with sweat, sap and sawdust.

Where the hell was she? He knew she needed time, space and whatever else to work through her feelings about him and about herself. But was the decision *that* hard? After so many hours had she decided he wasn't worth the risk?

Had she been turned off by his admittedly heavy-handed attempt to get through to her? Could she not see past his clumsy attempts to the honest depth of feeling that drove them?

Or was she not even *making* a decision? Maybe he'd read the entire situation wrong. Maybe she'd hitchhiked back to Boston to find another man who wouldn't ask so much. Maybe he hadn't gotten to her as deeply as he imagined—or maybe she'd been more afraid than he knew.

Maybe she'd meant what she said about being sick of men. Maybe she'd become a nun. Or a lesbian.

Maybe she'd gotten lost in the woods. Maybe she'd fallen and she couldn't get up…

Slate rolled his eyes and shut off his rattling brain. A mess. He was a god-awful jittery mess who'd cut enough firewood to last about seven years. If she didn't come back soon there'd be no forest left. Just piles of neatly cut logs, crushing the ferns and grasses underneath.

He trudged up the stairs and pulled on a clean pair of pants, a clean shirt, wanting to look decent when she returned. Just wanting her to return. He hadn't

felt this chewed up since he'd left Sue and gone overseas, since he'd gotten her letter saying that there was
someone else and thanks for the memories.

No woman had gotten to him that way until Rose.
Now here he was again, with his emotional fate in
female hands. He hated it. He hated it just as much
as the first time, if not more, now that he wasn't an
idealistic kid anymore. Now that he knew what he
could have and that he might want it with Rose.

Why couldn't he fall for some sweet, uncomplicated girl-next-door? Someone he could relax around,
have kids with, support in balancing family and career. Someone not plagued by demons, not afraid to
be herself. Someone who hadn't built a life around
working her way through the male population of Boston.

He was halfway down the stairs when he heard her
out in the woods, the steady tramp and crackle of
twigs and leaves compressed under her weight. He
made it down the stairs and stood facing the door,
knowing he looked like some ridiculous sentinel father and not caring. She'd come back. That simple
fact filled and stilled him into watchful silence.

She came in quietly, caught his eye and held it, her
gaze direct and questioning, a tremulous smile curv-
ing her mouth. All the makeup was gone from her
face, the careful mask stripped away. Something very,
very sweet and hopeful started singing in his brain.
She was ethereal; she glowed with inner light, like a
damn Christmas angel lawn ornament.

He was nuts about her.

She closed the door quietly behind her, folded her
hands, stood alone and vulnerable in front of the pale
pine walls like the sexiest version of pure innocence

he'd ever seen. He waited, wanting her to speak first, to confirm the transition he sensed and saw in her.

"My name is Alice Rose Katzenbaum. I was born in Normal, Illinois in 1975. My dad left when I was two. My mom took in whatever male company she could for as long as she could. I was a lonely kid, with not many friends, no dates. I survived by writing stories, ideas, journals, whatever I could put down on paper. I went to Boston when I was eighteen because I didn't know what else to do. I got a job as a secretary at Harvard and did freelance writing work— articles, stories—and found I was good at it. I also found I was as good as my mom with men, only I didn't let myself need them the way she did. I didn't let them have as much of me as she did. I kept the power to me, to myself. I worked hard for that. That was all-important." She faltered, looked away, then drew herself up and met his gaze again. "Until now."

He moved slowly toward her, unsure how to proceed, but determined to show how much her gift meant, that it was safe with him. "Rose…"

"This is me." She gestured clumsily, up and down her body. "This is me. I can't be any more 'me' than this. I don't know if it's what you want."

He swallowed the emotion in his throat. "Is it what *you* want?"

"Oh, Slate." She gave a tiny choked laugh and gestured helplessly. "You are relentless. Yes, it's what I want."

He reached for her, touched her smooth clean face, her clear natural skin, kissed her mouth, warm and soft and tasting of blackberries, kissed her again, gathered her close against him and laughed for the sheer joy of holding her, fresh and natural and willing in his arms.

"Alice Rose Katzenbaum." He tipped her face up and grinned into her fabulous unadorned, dark-lashed blue eyes. "You have no idea how good it is to finally meet you."

10

RILEY KNOCKED ON Melissa's door and moved restlessly; the paper surrounding the red roses cradled in his arms crackled loudly in the silent hall. He'd called her a few hours ago and suggested they meet in her apartment. The overly colorful anonymity of Rose's place had served its purpose in the beginning, but if he wanted Melissa to deal with the reality of the two of them together, he'd have to start by gently cutting away her safety nets. The pause on the other end of the line at his request had lengthened to ridiculous proportions before she grudgingly said okay.

Riley smiled now in her hall as he'd smiled at the sound of her acquiescence. Letting him into her apartment wasn't the same as letting him into her body or into her life, but it was a good starting point.

She opened the door with the smile that always seemed to chip part of him away and make it hers. Instantly he registered a change, and studied her harder to pinpoint the source. She wore a tiny black skirt that stretched across her thighs and molded to her hips the way he wanted to. Her off-white top was full and sleeveless and showed off the firm contours of her slender arms. Nothing new there. But something steely and determined sparked in her eyes; she sported new purpose and confidence in her bearing.

Intriguing, as most everything about her was.

"For you." He presented her with the roses, their color a vivid accent against her outfit.

"Oh, gosh. These are…" She blushed nearly the color of the flowers and sent him a bemused and speculative glance. "These are lovely. Thank you. I'll put them in water."

He grinned at her confusion, her embarrassment and the damn fabulous view of her thighs disappearing under the back of her skirt as she hurried to the kitchen. He moved into the living room, taking in the muted colors, the restrained elegance of the decor. About as different from Rose's riotous collection as you could get. More along the lines of his own place, now that he thought of it, but with a distinctly feminine flair.

Melissa returned from the kitchen, roses spilling out of a cut crystal vase, which she put on a side table. Their rich red color was like an intrusion into the neutral beige, gray and cream tones in the room. He'd chosen well.

Melissa stared at the flowers, glanced around her room as if she was seeing it for the first time, and gave a tiny shrug. "I love them. They're beautiful."

"Like you." He moved forward, drew his hands down her shoulders and bent until his lips were hovering over the smooth skin on her neck. The roses had done their job. He had to proceed slowly now, to show her with whatever means possible that she could want more from him than sex. Balance the romantic with the carnal. Little by little, advance and then retreat. Two steps forward, one back.

"Where do you want to do it?" He whispered the question into her skin, deliberately coarse, trying to keep her off balance, trusting in the end she'd get more of what she wanted than she knew how to ask for.

She stiffened, then relaxed and turned to face him, seductive confidence back in her eyes and movements.

"Bedroom." She pointed back over his shoulder. "That way."

He grinned, his body reacting already, reached and pulled her tight against him. "I'm ready."

"So I feel." She laughed and slid her arms around his neck. "Will you carry me in there, Tarzan? I've always wanted a guy to do that. My boyfriend tried once, but he nearly got a hernia and had to lie down for an hour with an ice pack."

"How romantic." Riley moved her hips, forward and back, loving the feel of her firm softness under his hands, reveling in a shameless testosterone rush at her faith in his strength. The woman could definitely make him feel like Superman. Now he wanted her to make him feel like Riley. "I think I can manage a little Tarzan. But without the yodeling."

She giggled and waited expectantly. He took her arms from around his neck, brought her wrists down and behind her back, pulled her up close and kissed her, slowly, softly, keeping the pressure sweet and gentle, keeping his tongue back against his teeth. A strange ache rose in him at the contact between their lips, like the empty feeling of oncoming grief mixed with a full fierce happiness.

Melissa pushed her head up and tried to increase the pressure, tried to loosen her hands from his grip. He resisted, pulled back and kissed her again. He wanted to keep the feeling going, wanted her to feel it, too. Lazy, tender, relentless kisses until she broke away and hid her face against his chest, her breath coming hard. Riley raised his head and for one eyes-squeezed-shut second hoped she felt what he did, that she wasn't just turned on, but shaken.

He released her wrists and swept her up into his arms, studying her face as he strode into the bedroom. She stared back, puzzled, curious.

"Why did you kiss me like that?"

He arched his eyebrows, deliberately obtuse. "Like what?"

"Like you just did." She gestured, exasperated, eyes darting up to meet his, then darting away. "Sort of…sweetly."

"Because I felt like it."

"Oh?"

"Oh." He lowered her onto the bed, knowing he was being irritating and enjoying himself hugely.

"You didn't kiss me at all last time."

He nodded, pleased she'd noticed. "Last time I didn't feel like it."

"Okay, okay." Melissa laughed and rolled her eyes.

He smiled, sat next to her and drew his finger across her mouth. "I have another present for you."

"Oooh!" She tilted her head and adopted a vapid bimbo stare. "*Diamonds?* Like, a t*iara?*"

He chuckled and bent close. "If I could think of something sexy to do with diamonds I'd buy them for you."

She stared at him, then laughed uneasily. "What is it?"

He made a show of reaching into his back pocket and drew out a thick, soft sable brush he'd bought from some hideously overpriced cosmetic store.

"Ooh." The syllable came out this time with genuine pleasure. "Time for *art* class, Teacher?"

He grinned. The woman delighted him. He wanted to capture her energy, her special joyous flavor, and hold it to him tightly. Bring her red flowers every day. Not let her waste herself on the boring jerk she thought she deserved, who didn't deserve her at all.

"Take your clothes off."

She moved on the bed; her eyes darkened; she swallowed.

"You first," she whispered.

He shook his head, met and held her challenging gaze. "I'm the teacher, remember?"

She lay still for a moment longer, then nodded, though he didn't sense an ounce of real surrender. She sat up and pulled off the sleeveless sweater; her breasts were full and unexpectedly naked underneath. His breath drew in; his hands moved to touch her before he was aware of the instinct and checked it. Not yet. He pulled his hands back down beside him. Not until she had tired of the brush, tired of playing, and was ready to admit out loud that she wanted him to make love to her because she felt that deeply about him.

She lay back, lifted her hips and slid the skirt slowly down, revealing her stomach, then the naked mound of her sex. This time his hands grabbed fistfuls of the bedspread.

Melissa lifted her chin and smiled proudly. "Thought I'd save time."

He grinned, using every trick of mind control in his vast arsenal to keep from shedding his own clothes and stretching out on top of her.

"Very efficient." To his relief, his voice came out

smooth and natural, not the strained croak he feared. "Close your eyes and lie still."

She settled back, eyes closed, body expectantly tense. He sat beside her in the curve of her waist and drew the brush across her mouth. Her lips twitched into a smile; she giggled.

"Shh." He painted her beautiful features, across her eyelids, down her nose, across her cheeks and forehead, using a light feathering touch. Her face relaxed, the tension went out of her forehead, from around her eyes and mouth.

He drew the brush down her throat, followed the lines of her collarbone and shoulders, explored the length of her arm, painted each finger with slow, careful strokes, keeping the task technical and precise in his mind, so he wouldn't have to think about how pathetic it was to be jealous of a clump of dead animal hair.

"Mmm. Nice." Her voice was low, dreamy. He moved the brush to her breast, painted up from her chest, increasing the pressure slightly, down and up from the edge to the aureole in the center, covering the fullness on each side.

She squirmed and arched her upper body. He paused, let her wait for a few tantalizing seconds, then circled the brush around her nipple, using the tip, the textured cut bristles in a slow, thorough sweep.

"How does that feel?" He didn't need to ask; he could read it in her face, in her body. But he wanted to hear her voice, to sense if she would get to the point of turning away from the games, to him.

"Like the softest touch you can imagine." She opened her eyes. "Do you want to try?"

He shook his head and put gentle fingers to her eyes to close them again. "Not yet."

Not until she accepted him as a real lover. He moved down the bed to sit by her legs, and swept the damn lucky brush down her stomach, outlining her navel, then lower to circle the dark cluster of hair. She opened for him, eager for the kiss of the bristles between her legs.

He gritted his teeth and made her wait, traveled down both legs, eliciting moans of pleasure when he stroked the brush on her feet, then back up to tease the skin of her inner thighs. She shifted, lifted her hips so her sex was spread open to him. Riley closed his eyes and beat back the primal urge to throw the brush out the window and take her as nature intended—as their natures intended.

"Riley?" Her voice was soft and thick. She lifted her head and stared at him, questioning. He held her gaze, loathing this spectator role, letting her see in his eyes everything he wanted to do to her.

"What do you want, Melissa?" He let the question fall gently into the silence between them, imbued it with meaning she could take or leave.

Her eyes flashed wide; her mouth opened to speak. He imagined her saying "You." Imagined it so hard he could almost hear the word. He stared intently, willing her to admit what he desperately wanted her to be feeling.

She pointed to the brush in his hand. "I want that. I want you to make me come with it. Then I want to do it to you."

He averted his eyes so she wouldn't see his disappointment, pushed her legs open wider and stroked the brush up the center of her sex. Like an artist he dipped into her; her moisture clung to the soft bristles. He painted her, concentrating on her center of pleasure, dipped again and stroked her, light lapping strokes of the brush.

It was killing him.

She moaned and shifted. Her hips came up. Receded. Up and down. She shook her head wildly, shook it again. Reached an arm, found his shoulder and tugged him up toward her.

"Riley."

"Yes." His heart leaped; he increased the speed of his stroking, wanting to provoke her into an admission. "What is it?"

She reached for him again and pulled harder. Let go. Pulled him again.

He turned his body to stone, slowed the brush to keep her from her climax. *Come on, Melissa.* "Tell me."

"No." She put her hands back over her face. "Nothing. Keep going. Keep going."

"What is it? What do you want?" He strained toward her, halting the brush strokes, keeping the urgency from his voice as best he could.

"Just…keep going."

"That's all?"

"Yes." The word came out false and desperate. "Yes."

He leaned forward so his head came level with her breasts, so he could hear the short shallow breaths she took. "Do you want me to make love to you, Melissa?"

Her body went absolutely still. She brought her hands down from her face and stared at him, eyes large and wary. "Why did you ask me that?"

"Because I want to know. Because I think you might."

She swallowed convulsively, still staring at him as if he might turn into her worst nightmare. "No. No, I don't."

Bull. He lunged over her and pressed her down into the mattress, kissed her mouth hard with real passion, rocked between her legs. "No? You don't want this? Don't want to feel me inside you?"

"No." She sounded miserable, close to tears. "This was supposed to be—"

"I know what it was supposed to be." He kissed her face, her mouth. Why was she fighting him so hard? "Why can't it change if we both want it to?"

"I don't want change. I like things as they are."

He pulled back, looked hard into her face. "I can't believe that."

"Riley, please…"

"Are you afraid?" He put his hand to her heart, risking it all. "Afraid of what you might feel if I make love to you?"

She closed her eyes and shook her head. "Don't do this."

Triumph swelled in him, along with piercing tenderness. "Oh, Melissa. I *wouldn't* do this if I didn't think it would satisfy you so much more than all these toys you want me to use on you."

She opened her eyes and looked at him, her expression unreadable. Not the glowing surrender he'd fantasized about seeing, but not the opposite, either. Almost as if she were making up her mind about something he had no part in.

Suddenly, she pushed him over onto his back, her face clear, the confidence returned. Whatever she'd been thinking about, she'd obviously decided. And with her hands unbuttoning his shirt and running over his chest, Riley was pretty damn sure he liked her decision.

He lay back, allowing her free rein over his body. She seemed to be lit with some kind of female fire, as if their times together had transformed her into the pure expression of sensuality she'd wanted to explore.

She was magnificent. He had to fight to keep from making her his in the most arrogant male way possible. This was her moment. Let her be in charge for a while. He'd get his turn.

She kissed his chest, pulled his arm out of his shirt sleeve and brought it up over his head so his hand bumped something soft draped over the headboard. She held it there, kissed a line of kisses up his arm toward his hand. He closed his eyes, savoring the feel of her warm mouth on his biceps, his forearm, his wrist. Through the erotic haze, he became aware of something cold and metallic against his wrist, then heard a click and felt the chill of metal against his skin.

Caught.

His adrenaline kicking in, he reached up with his other hand behind her head to test the strength of the bond. "What the—"

Click. Other hand. Caught.

Melissa's face came into view, cheeks flushed, eyes shining. Half scared, half triumphant, as if she didn't really believe what she'd done.

Neither did he.

"What the hell is this, Melissa?" He spoke in a low even tone to hide the fact that he was seriously rattled. He didn't like being made helpless, especially by the one woman who had already managed to put such a dent in his self-control.

"This is payback time."

He watched her face carefully, trying not to think about that movie where Kathy Bates tortured a male hostage tied to her bed. He didn't think Melissa had anything that twisted in her. "For what?"

She leaned forward and drew her warm, lingering tongue across his nipples. "All the pleasure you've given me."

His body tensed, started to sweat; he tested the strength of the metal against his wrists. Not too strong, probably toy. He might be able to break one.

Melissa's hands slipped down his stomach and fumbled with the fly of his pants, unsnapped, unzipped. Then her fingers were on him, warm and insistent—on, then under the cotton of his briefs. He started to lose it.

"Melissa, don't do this." His voice came out a hoarse whisper. This wasn't what he'd planned. He was supposed to seduce her, give her pleasure. If she let him make love to her he could be there with her. They could go over the edge together. But not this way. Not with him tied here, victim to the stroking of her fingers, torn by excitement and dread. Defenseless short of physical force, which not even the most dire circumstances would get him to use against her.

"It's the only way you'll let me."

"Untie me and we can be in it together."

"No." She kissed her way down his stomach, to the open fly of his jeans, then kissed along the hard length of him. "I want to do *this*."

He flinched, strained against the metal binding him,

fighting the pleasure of her lips and tongue. This wasn't what he wanted, not this way. "Melissa."

She crawled down to crouch between his legs, and applied herself in earnest. Her warm mouth moved up and down; her hands cupped him, caressed him underneath.

He yanked on the chains, hoping to snap the metal, but it held. He hated this, hated the vulnerability, hated that he might lose the battle and give himself to her this way, without making her admit she wanted him inside her.

He stared at the ceiling, trying to shut out the pleasure and concentrate. But the sensations, the heat, the wetness of her mouth permeated every thought, every attempt to keep her away. He hated most the part of him that wanted her to keep going, to take everything from him, to wear down the barrier he'd erected. The one she was stripping away with her mouth and tongue, reducing him to the basest form of his own humanity.

Exactly as he'd tried to do to her.

God, what a pompous ass he was. Thinking he was the master, thinking he could teach her all about herself with his superior knowledge and skill. She'd turned the tables on him in the instant it took to snap cuffs on his wrists. Now all that was left him to save face, to hide his vulnerability, was to hang on, not give in.

Her mouth slid up to the tip of his erection and came off. A tortured sigh-groan escaped him. He closed his eyes, hoping by blocking out the sight of her he could hang on to the dregs of his control and his pride, aware by now he was fighting a losing battle.

She bent and licked him, tiny gentle flicks up, bottom to the top, then settled her mouth firmly back on him and he was gone. He lifted his hips into her rhythm, yanked against the chains until a final powerful tug snapped one.

"No." He reached down, grabbed under her armpit and dragged her up beside him. He pushed onto her belly once, twice, and spilled shamefully onto her skin, shuddering in unwelcome ecstasy.

Damn. Damn her. Damn him. Damn everything. He lay there, spent, beaten, humiliated. She'd ripped him wide-open, left him nothing to cover himself with.

"Riley..."

"Shh."

She tried to struggle free but he held her head against his chest. He had to marshal his control, find some shred of shielding he could use to protect himself. She'd cheated them both. Rejected his offer and made him part of her game, when he'd been so sure deep down she wanted more.

"Riley." She managed to wriggle free of his restraining arm and looked up into his face, searching, bewildered. He stared back, utterly unable to summon his trademark mask of indifference.

She caught her lower lip between her teeth. "Oh God, Riley, I'm...I thought you'd... It was supposed to be fun."

"It was fine." The wooden words left his lips and made her wince.

"No." She sat up. "It wasn't. You looked at me like I was the next Lorena Bobbitt."

He rolled off the bed, fastened his pants, took two tissues and tossed them to her to wipe off her stomach. He wanted to get away from her, go somewhere he could regroup, regain some balance, do something ridiculously male, like pick a fight with a professional kickboxer. "I better go."

"No!" She jumped off the bed, came over to him and grabbed his arms. "No. Please. Not until we can straighten this out."

"Straighten what out? It's all pretty damn clear to me."

"Riley—"

His cell phone rang. He pushed Melissa gently away and retrieved it from his pocket.

"Riley, it's Karen."

His muscles tensed at the sound of his sister's tearful voice. "What is it?"

"Leo's...something's really wrong. I'm taking him to the emergency room at Children's Hospital. Can you meet me?"

"I'll be there right away." He punched off the phone, gut twisting in fear.

"Riley. What happened?"

"My nephew's at the hospital. I have to go." He looked at her, standing in front of him, naked and beautiful, her eyes wide with alarm for a child she didn't know, and he made a decision without even realizing he'd been deciding.

"Come with me."

11

MELISSA SAT in the waiting room at Children's Hospital beside Riley and Karen, hands clenched, floating in that bizarre space between total agonizing tension and bone-melting exhaustion. They'd been waiting over an hour already while little Leo underwent an emergency appendectomy. If moments like these defined parenthood, there was no way she could manage it with her sanity intact.

After she'd agreed to go with him, Riley and Melissa had driven to the hospital in silence, Riley gripping the wheel, face set in grim, determined lines. Melissa had watched the city go by, shaken, helpless to know how to comfort him, still mortified by the way her supposedly empowering decision to take matters into her own...mouth, had backfired.

Simply put, she'd panicked. He'd thrown her completely, first with those endless sweet kisses that practically had her exploding with emotions too powerful and frightening to name, then by being so insistent that they make love. As if he could read her mind, see all the unwelcome feelings and longings that consumed her while he stroked her with the softness of the brush. Out of her sexual arousal had sprung a yearning so deep she'd barely been able to fight it. A yearning to have him over and inside her, a yearning to reach her climax with him, surrounded by the warmth and strength of his body.

But then what? Once she'd given herself to Riley that way, there'd be no easy departure. No *hey, thanks for the orgasm, that was swell, see ya later.* After an experience like that she'd be gone. Lost. Sex Goddess Melissa trampled to death under the onslaught of her own ordinary-woman emotions. And he'd have the right to look surprised and say, "I thought this was only about sex. What is it with you chicks?"

Only thank God Riley wouldn't use a word like *chicks.*

The door to the outside hall opened; parents all around the room stiffened and fixed attentive, hopeful gazes toward it. A doctor came out and spoke to a nearby couple. Their son was going to be okay. The surgeons had been able to remove the mass completely; no, it wasn't cancerous. The woman broke down and embraced her husband. The husband shook the doctor's hand, tears streaming from his eyes.

Melissa shrank back into her chair, feeling like slugs were a step above her in the evolutionary chain. While these people had been facing life and death, stretched to the limits of endurance and hope, she'd been playing. Manipulating. Toying with someone and spitting all over her true feelings.

How much longer would she go on thinking of herself as some kind of wild woman in the face of endless evidence that she didn't have what it took?

When they'd arrived at the hospital and rushed inside to meet Karen and Leo, Riley had enveloped his sister in a strong, comforting hug that reduced Karen to tears she'd probably managed to keep back before then. Melissa had stood awkwardly to one side, unable to take her eyes off him—no longer Riley, Stud for Hire, but a warm, protective older brother, concerned and scared and trying to be strong for his family. It was suddenly and hopelessly impossible to keep pretending this was about sex with a stranger.

Beside her, Riley crossed and recrossed his legs; his sister flipped pages of a magazine, obviously not reading. Melissa cleared her throat, hoping in some small way to be able to ease the tension. "Waiting is the worst."

Riley nodded. "Though in my line of work, you get used to it."

His words sank in slowly, along with their significance. She hadn't a clue what he did. Who he was. Where he lived. She had a sudden, ravenous need to know, to ground him in serious, responsible reality. So instead of imagining him flying through the air saving the universe, she could think of him during the day in a nice suit, on the phone, sharpening pencils and dictating memos. Things she could relate to. Things that might even make a real relationship between them seem not so far out of reach.

"What do you do?" She blushed, keeping her voice low so his sister wouldn't hear. Kind of a strange question, considering they'd been rolling around naked a few hours before.

He smiled as if her question pleased him, but hesitated before he answered. "I'm a private investigator."

"Oh?" Her nine-to-five corporate fantasy was in jeopardy. "You mean like 'is my husband faithful' and 'who's taking the company toilet paper?' Stuff like that?"

He shook his head, his eyes measuring her reaction. "Usually not quite that tame."

"You mean like...murders and kidnappings?" Melissa winced. For heaven's sake, she sounded like a squeaky teenager who watched too much TV. Of *course* he didn't—

"Would that upset you?"

Her jaw dropped. "I don't...I mean—"

"It's not usually that grisly. A lot of it is pretty dull. But it can get...involved sometimes." He still watched her carefully, though his voice was matter-of-fact, as if he was sharing a favorite chili recipe.

"But...don't the police usually handle criminal stuff?" Her sentence ended in a wistful squeak. Couldn't he have been an accountant? Or a financial consultant? Someone who sat in an office for eight hours a day and came home to take the family out to KFC for dinner. Someone who'd share her dream of kids and the PTA and family game night. Someone who'd think plain old non-Sex Goddess Melissa was exciting and fabulous and worth building a life with.

"Some of my clients don't want the police involved, at least at first. Sometimes the police come to me for help." His lips tightened for a fraction of a second. "They have to operate by the book, which can be...inconvenient sometimes."

Melissa nodded; a sick feeling sank like a boulder into her stomach. Here she was, finally ready to admit she wanted the games over with, and the reality had turned out to be even more fantastic than the fantasy. Just when she'd started to allow herself hope that Riley could be a real friend and lover, she found out he was James Bond.

She squinted at him; her stunned brain struggled to

make sense of something. Riley. In Rose's apartment. All those noises.

"So that's why…" Her voice rose from its careful whisper. "That's why you were going through Rose's underwear."

His sister closed her magazine and rolled her eyes. "No offense, but I don't think I need to hear this, though in his business there's usually a logical explanation." She stood and raked red-nailed fingers through her dark permed hair. "Decaf, anyone? I can't stand just sitting here."

"No, thanks." Melissa smiled, admiring Karen's poise and courage, wishing they could have met under other circumstances, when her son wasn't in danger and when Melissa's mind was actually functioning.

Riley shook his head; his sister kissed his forehead and ruffled his hair before she went out the door, her steps nervous and jerky.

Melissa stared at Riley, his tousled hair, the red lipstick mark on his face. She was having a very, very hard time with this. Except that maybe even James Bond was someone's little brother.

"So you were investigating Rose?"

He shrugged. "In a way."

Melissa's stomach twisted in sympathy for Rose. Poor thing. No wonder she'd wanted to escape. She couldn't even trust one of her own friends. "What kind of way?"

"I can't tell you."

"Of course. I'm sorry." She gave a small sad smile. A P.I. In retrospect, it made perfect sense. His constant air of caution, of holding back, observing. The natural inclination to keep his thoughts and feelings to himself. No wonder she couldn't relax entirely around him. No wonder she felt like a butterfly on stickpins when he looked at her.

He had a whole life, an entire existence she couldn't possibly understand or appreciate or be part of. Sneaky, subversive, flirting with the wrong side of the law when necessary. Lying would come easily to him, manipulation, possibly even violence. He probably owned a gun and knew how to use it. What the hell did she know about any of that? What use would he have for a woman like her?

No wonder he'd taken the handcuffs so hard. What was a game to her was probably serious business to him. He was a tough man, doing a probably dangerous job, and she was in marketing, for God's sake. It was like pairing a guerilla fighter with Martha Stewart.

Hi, honey, did you liberate any countries from oppressive dictatorships today? Oh, good. While you were gone I made a fabulous seasonal centerpiece out of those old hand grenades you had in the garage....

This was agony.

Except there was the way he'd kissed her early that night, right after he arrived at her apartment, before her awful miscalculation had ruined things. And the way he'd hugged his sister when they met at the emergency room. And the way he'd looked after they wheeled his nephew out of sight on the gurney. Vulnerable. Scared. Totally human.

"What do *you* do?" He leaned forward and brushed her hair off her face. "When you're not tying men to your bed?"

"Oh...I'm assistant marketing director at the museum of art. I come up with ways to make our exhibits as appealing as possible to the public, develop edu-

cation programs for school groups and...*et cetera.*"
She nearly laughed at the inane sound of her answer.
"And...I'm sorry about the handcuffs. It seemed like
a fun, sexy idea when I had it."

He edged forward in his seat and leaned toward
her, eyes still hauntingly magnetic, even ringed with
fatigue and strain. "It *was* a fun, sexy idea, Melissa.
But it didn't work for one important reason."

She bit her lip, preparing for the inevitable lashing.
"Which you're going to tell me."

"Because it wasn't what either of us wanted to be
doing." His voice came out low, husky and seductive;
he touched her cheek, a warm, gentle touch that made
her battered hopes awaken again. "The next time
we're in bed together it's going to be you and me.
No games. No toys."

"No toys?" His sister sat back down with her coffee.

Easily, naturally, Riley shifted around to include
Karen in the conversation. "I was just telling Melissa
that the dresser I'm making for Leo needs sprucing
up a little."

A cold shiver made the rounds of Melissa's skeletal
structure. He didn't blink. Didn't miss a beat. His
expression, his demeanor and his voice had changed
smoothly, in an instant. Talking about sex to talking
about furniture. Press a button and switch personali-
ties. As he must have done when she'd caught him
going through Rose's drawers and he'd claimed he
was looking for underwear.

"Oh?" His sister put down her coffee and stared
at him thoughtfully. "I thought you said it was perfect."

"It's not...six-year-old enough. It needs something more fun. Less...square."

"*Really.*" Karen flicked a glance over to Melissa, then back to Riley. "What an interesting development. Have you seen it yet, Melissa?"

"I...no. Not yet." She stumbled over the words, felt herself blush outrageously. She obviously hadn't benefited from years of practice lying. "But Riley has, uh, told me about it and how, you know, square he thinks it is."

"Well." Karen continued to stare speculatively, the hint of a smile at the corners of her mouth. "Sounds like you might be the right person to help him liven it up."

Riley sent his sister a boyish grin. "I think you're right."

Melissa swallowed, slightly disoriented. Did she miss something? Did this piece of furniture have tremendous significance she should know about?

She suddenly wanted out of the hospital, away from this man, back to the quiet comforting predictability of Bill. Bill's honesty was so much a part of him that he hadn't even been able to start dating someone else after they broke up without telling her about it. So, he was a little dull. At least he didn't know how to shoot people. And she couldn't ever remember being wildly confused around him. Not even vaguely bewildered. And she'd never once caught him going through someone else's underwear. Those were things she admired in a man. Required, even.

A handsome young doctor dressed in green scrubs, came through the door and headed toward them.

Karen, Riley and Melissa stood abruptly for the endless seconds it took him to approach.

He smiled reassuringly, his eyes crinkling behind his glasses. "The surgery went fine. We'll keep Leo here a few days so we can keep him comfortable and on antibiotics. I anticipate he'll be back to his old self in a week or so."

"Oh, thank God. Riley." Karen flew to her brother, laughing and crying all at once.

Melissa let out breath she didn't know she'd been holding and practically hurt her face smiling. She watched Riley, his arms around Karen, his face clenched with a fierce combination of love, joy and relief.

Her smile died; her heart and throat squeezed painfully. The more she was with this man, the more she wanted him, the more conflicted and difficult it was to be around him and the more out of reach he seemed. That wasn't how it was supposed to be. Real love grew quietly, rose naturally out of shared time and experiences, shared values and backgrounds.

Riley opened his eyes and grinned at her over his sister's head. Melissa gave a silly, inadequate thumbs-up and managed to grin back, feeling sick and exhausted and confused.

No matter how sexy and fabulous Riley made her seem when they were in bed together, no matter how powerful and exciting her infatuation with him was, he wasn't the right man for her. She wasn't the right woman for him. It was time to let the dream go and face the reality of who she was and what she wanted.

The adventure had to end.

"WELL, *I* THINK THE QUEEN should have told old whatsisname to get lost, and annulled the forced marriage to Viola so Viola and Will could have lived happily ever after." Penny plunked her empty popcorn bowl on the coffee table. "I hate sad endings. I mean, if I want to see suffering and misery, all I have to do is turn on the news. I go to movies to *escape* all that."

Melissa stopped the tape of *Shakespeare in Love* and pressed the rewind button. "I don't know. Viola is probably better off. After all that exciting Romeo and Juliet, forbidden-love stuff wore off she and Will might have found out they weren't meant for each other, after all. I mean, you can't really know you're in love by the way someone looks and how they kiss."

Penny stared at her in astonishment. "You don't believe in love at first sight?"

"Absolutely not." Melissa banished the image of Riley that first time she'd opened Rose's door to him. Yes, the feelings had been powerful, the attraction explosive, but that wasn't *love.*

Penny shook her head. "You probably would have smacked Will away after the first meeting and stopped the movie in its tracks."

"No. But I wouldn't have expected forever based on that initial thrill. At least with the gross husband Viola isn't in for any huge disappointments. And maybe he'll turn out to be better than she thinks."

Penny lowered her glasses and turned pitying eyes on Melissa. "Why are you so sure that you can't have passion *and* marriage together?"

"You can, I guess. But wild passionate feelings aren't enough to build a life together. Those feelings come from insecurity or desperation, not real love.

Real love is what's left after all that other gaga stuff wears off.''

''You sound like you're trying very hard to convince yourself, Miss Melissa. Does this have anything to do with Bill the Snore-man versus Tom-Riley, Double-oh-seven?''

Melissa attempted a casual shrug. ''Possibly.''

''Geez, Melissa, has it ever occurred to you that most guys are more fun than Bill and considerably less exhausting than your James Bond guy? How can you base a theory on such a small statistical sample?''

''Because it's true. Look at me. I'm on some crazy addictive high for this guy. He's all I think about, all I want all day long.'' Her voice thickened. ''I cry when I talk about him, I pine, I giggle, I'm a total crazy person. It's ridiculous.''

Penny froze in a dramatic mouth-open position. ''Oh. My. God. You're in love with him.''

''No.'' Melissa pushed away a mutinous affirmative thrill. ''That's just the *point*. This isn't love. This is…mental illness.''

Penny slumped onto Melissa's sofa and clutched a pillow to her stomach. ''This is a disaster, is what it is. You really know how to pick 'em.''

''Penny, I have not picked him. More to the point, he's not even close to picking me.''

''Are you going to keep seeing him?''

''Once more. To break it off.'' Her face crumpled and she took a deep fortifying breath. She was *not* going to cry over him. Nor was she going to admit how deeply she felt about him, especially to Penny and maybe not even to herself.

''Case closed.'' Penny shook her head mournfully. ''You're in love.''

"How can I possibly be in love when all we've done is kinky stuff? I've never even had a conversation with the man." She wrinkled her nose. "Well, not many. Not *enough.*"

"What's enough?"

"Enough to know him. To know what he's like in different moods. When he's angry, when he—"

"You've seen him angry."

"Okay, yes." She put her hands up in surrender. "We've done angry. To know how he handles stress, how he reacts in a, uh…"

"Crisis?" Penny shot her a know-it-all glance. "Did we not find ourselves in the emergency room last night?"

"*Yes.* Okay. Fine. But there's the small fact that he confuses me hopelessly and we're totally unsuited. And another thing." She found herself pacing the floor, and stopped in the middle of a crazy-woman gesture to avoid making Penny look any more smug. "Regardless of how I feel, there is no way a guy that amazing would want someone like me. He's a total stud, for one. He's been around the world, he lives closer to the edge every day than I'd want to in my worst nightmare. I mean, what the hell does a woman like me have to offer him?"

"Gee, I don't know, maybe low self-esteem?" Penny snorted. "If anything, you're too good for him. You're twice the woman he is, Melissa. You just don't know it."

Melissa gave a wry smile. "You think? *Twice* the woman?"

"You know what I mean." Penny waved her hands dismissively. "You're in love with him. Admit it and then we can decide what to do."

"I'm *not* in love—" Melissa gave a strangled groan and collapsed on her couch. *Oh, help.* It was hopeless. Why bother trying to fool herself any longer? "Okay, I'm in love with him."

"Good for you." Penny applauded heartily. "The first step in treating any illness is to diagnose it. Now are you *sure* this man has no feelings for you?"

"I don't know." Melissa gestured wearily, totally drained by the admission. "Sometimes I think he—"

A knock sounded on Melissa's door. Not Riley's confident rapping, but a timid excuse-me knock. Melissa shrugged at Penny's questioning look and walked over to the door.

"Who is it?" She raised her voice and bent her head close to hear the answer.

"My name is Amanda." A deep female voice came through the wood. "I'm a friend of Rose's."

Penny giggled. "Ah! Amanda of No-Last-Name. Close personal friend of Tom-slash-Riley. Enabler of sex lessons for Rose, who of course turned out to be Melissa. How I have longed to meet her!"

Melissa made a not-very-polite gesture behind her back at Penny, to hide her attack of nerves, and swung the door open. A young, attractive women with a giant mane of red hair stood on the threshold wearing skintight clothes and a worried frown.

"Sorry to bother you, but I just wondered if you'd seen your neighbor across the hall in the last week or so. Her name is Rose."

"No." Melissa smiled politely, wondering if Riley had told Amanda about her. Wondering if Amanda knew Riley was investigating Rose. Wondering how her life ever got this complicated. "I think she said she was going away."

"It's not like Rose to leave without saying something. No one's talked to her since she was supposed to meet a friend of mine on a blind date."

"Oh?" Melissa swallowed. She bet she knew who that friend was. So Riley hadn't told Amanda they'd been seeing each other.

"Tom and I are starting to get really worried." The woman held out her hands, nails ragged with chipped pink polish. "I'm a manicurist and look what I've done to myself. And Tom said he hasn't given a decent haircut in three days."

A loud gasp sounded from behind Melissa, which would have echoed her own, but hers had jammed in her throat. She shook her head to clear it, which merely rattled her brain and made her slightly dizzy. "Haircut?"

"Yeah. Tom's a stylist. We work together. But he's not...you know." She extended a limp wrist. "Hardly."

Melissa stared blankly. Was Riley going undercover as a—

"I knew it!" Penny's horrified moan made Melissa wince. "He's a fake."

"What...does Tom...look like?" Melissa enunciated each word carefully. Her entire world was about to explode, and she didn't want to die mumbling.

"Oh, he's a total stud. Not real tall, not real big, but with to-die-for muscles, blue eyes, thick blond hair, the whole package." She studied Melissa curiously. "Why?"

Melissa shut her mouth, which had been gaping in horror. *Tom wasn't Riley. Which meant Riley wasn't Tom. Which meant she had no idea where he had come from or what he wanted from her.* "I just…thought I might have seen him…around."

"Not likely." Amanda looked behind her into the corridor, as if she was afraid of being overheard, and leaned closer. "Some thug cornered Tom the night of the date and told him not to come near Rose. Tom was pretty scared and he's no chicken. He said he was sure the guy was a *mobster* or something."

Another gasp, this one louder. Melissa grabbed the doorjamb to root herself on the rug that was threatening to be pulled out from under her. What had Riley's sister said? There was usually a logical explanation in his business. Of course, there must be. So Riley wasn't Tom; that didn't mean he wasn't who he said. Well, it did, but not necessarily in a bad way. Right?

She put her hands to her temples. Riley had warned Tom away that night and come himself so he could investigate Rose, and he got Melissa instead. That still worked. Right? Nothing she had to stretch too far to understand. Nothing inherently menacing. Maybe to Riley's surprise, he'd been attracted to Melissa and kept seeing her in spite of the mistake. Maybe he was just withholding details until the investigation was over. Client-detective privilege. Or something.

That could happen. Right?

"Are you okay?" Amanda put a friendly arm on Melissa's shoulder.

"I'm fine. Fine." Her voice came out shaky, as if she'd been pounding down cappuccino all day long.

"I asked the cops to come by and meet me here. In case something happened to Rose." Amanda bit her lip apprehensively. "You haven't noticed any strange smells in the hall, have you?"

Melissa recoiled. "No...no—"

The elevator doors at the end of the hall opened. A large man who looked like he spent his free time exercising his beer-and-fries muscle came striding down the hall. He did not look happy.

"Police, Captain Watson. Which of you is Amanda?" He held up a badge and glanced from Amanda to Melissa. His eyes were a peculiar pale shade of blue that put Melissa further on edge. But at least she could be blissfully sure he was on the right side of the law.

"I'm her." Amanda patted her considerable chest. "I need you to break down my friend Rose's door and see if she's lying there dead. No one's heard from her in over a week."

The policeman grew slowly red in the face; a thick vein stood out in his forehead. He fumbled in his shirt pocket and came up with a roll of antacids, which he waved toward Melissa. "You live here?"

Melissa nodded.

"You haven't seen her, either?" He popped three tablets into his mouth.

Melissa shook her head. "Last we spoke, last week, she said she was leaving town for a while."

"What?" The policeman nearly choked on his medicine. He recovered with an effort and a chilling look spread over his face, as if he was itching to get his huge hands on a certain neck. "Any of you seen a guy hanging around? Tall, dark hair, brown eyes, solid build? Good-looking guy, about thirty-five."

Melissa's eyes widened; she swallowed convulsively. The cop's pale eyes darted to her. "You've seen him."

"I...well, I—"

"Yes." Penny came up behind her. "She's seen him. A bunch of times. Is he dangerous?"

"Penny, for heaven's sake." Melissa elbowed her friend in the stomach. The last thing she needed was for Penny's love of melodrama to get Riley in trouble.

The cop's face grew redder and more murderous. "But no sign of Rose? He hasn't been meeting Rose at her place?"

"No." Penny nudged Melissa's rib cage. "Tell him."

"I…" Melissa's throat closed around the words. The policeman pinned her with an unpleasant stare. She had the feeling that along with his beer and fries he devoured small children. "Well, he's been see-ing…me."

Air exploded out of the cop's mouth in an angry rush, followed by an impressive string of curses that scented the hall with peppermint antacids. The women stared at him in surprise. He suddenly appeared to notice and brought himself under control.

"Listen to me." He put a heavy hand on Melissa's shoulder. "This guy is extremely dangerous. We've been after him for some time."

"Oh my *God*. Melissa!" Penny squeaked.

Melissa gaped at the policeman, seeing various unconnected images of Riley. Mysterious. Powerful. Intense. But dangerous?

"I want you to sit down right now, all of you, and tell me everything he told you, everything he's done. Everything you know about this Rose person and where she might have gone." The cop pointed a beefy finger into Melissa's face. "And if he shows himself again around here, I want you to call me immediately, you understand? Don't let him in. Don't let him near

you. Get to the phone and call me. Rose, too. I want
to know anything you can find out about her, about
where she is.''

"Oh!" Penny clapped her hands to her face. ''I
knew they were bad news, both of them. I knew it. I
should have stopped you.''

"What has Riley done?" The words came from
Melissa's throat in a pleading rush. Whatever it was,
it couldn't be that bad. Maybe he'd skipped the fine
print on a couple of laws in pursuit of hardened criminals? Gotten a few too many parking tickets? Jay-
walked?

"I don't want to scare you, ma'am. The best thing
you can do is tell me everything.''

"I need to know." She gripped the soft flesh of
the policeman's forearm, barely aware of what she
was doing, and looked up into his face. "I need to
know what he did.''

The policeman wiped a hand through his thinning
hair and sighed, as if he were about to perform the
most unpleasant of duties. "He's a sociopath.''

Penny stifled a scream. Amanda gasped. Melissa
jerked her hands back from the policeman's arm and
stared, feeling the blood drain from her face, while
her mind tried to float off somewhere calm and safe
where his words couldn't reach her.

"He makes nice to women, gets them into bed, gets
what he wants for a while." The huge man leaned
forward, his puffy face lined with concern and regret.
"And then he kills them.''

Rose at top.

12

ROSE STRETCHED OUT on the ledge, blissfully enjoying the astonishing spread of stars overhead. The warmth of the blanket she'd brought down competed pleasantly with the chill night air for control of her body temperature. The water made luscious lapping sounds down on the rocky shore. Bats darted overhead, blanking out tiny patches of stars with their dark shapes. Could any more perfect day exist?

She wiggled her head into a more comfortable position on the hard rock. Only one thing could have made the day more perfect. If she'd been able to wake up with Slate this morning. Or if he was here right now, under the blanket making love to her instead of up at the house making late-night phone calls to his business contacts abroad.

Since the day she'd come clean with him about her past, their time together had been amazing. So easy, so calm, so right. Rose felt she could look far into her future and see him there at every turn, every twist of whatever her fate might be. She couldn't imagine a time when she wouldn't like him, wouldn't respect him, wouldn't trust him with her life. Even in the moments he would drive her crazy, as was inevitable with any couple, those three ingredients would last.

Put quite simply, she was in love, and the fact amazed her. Whoever would have thought little Alice

Rose Katzenbaum would grow up to be someone like Rose, and that Rose would grow up and blossom back into Alice Rose Katzenbaum? Whoever would have thought, after her long and checkered history, that a *man* would be the one to bring her back? A man with an easy grin and tough determination to win her trust, to make it safe for her true self to come out of hiding.

Whoever would have thought someone like her would ever be lying here, contemplating her very own happily ever after?

A streak of brilliant light crossed a portion of the sky—a shooting star. She gasped with pleasure and wished Slate had been there to share it, then to make her gasp with even more pleasure. Why the hell wasn't he? Everything between them was so right, except this strange absence of passion. She was on fire all day long just watching him. When he touched her she nearly combusted. But Slate?

Sometimes she'd look up and catch him staring, see the hunger in his eyes for the brief second before he masked it. Sometimes she'd feel his body aroused when he kissed her. But in spite of her not very subtle efforts to make him lose control, he'd put her firmly away and mumble something about a time and a place for everything.

As her friend Amanda would say, "What was up with that?" Rose was ready to swim out to a passing boat and beg a lobsterman to service her.

She grinned and waved away a mosquito whining close to her ear. As if. Amazingly, instinctively, she knew she couldn't desire anyone else. Maybe never would. Not this way. Not in a way that energized her and gave her peace at the same time. Not when there was a guy who'd glance up from his breakfast and grin, with a shine of butter and a sprinkle of crumbs on his mouth, and make her wild for him. Even in the little everyday things he enchanted her, obsessed her, made her crazy with a longing that went much deeper than the physical.

So what *was* up with that?

The shrill beep of Slate's cell phone carried down to the shore through the woods. Rose grimaced. Nothing like spending all this time away from civilization to make you aware of how often, and with what ugliness, it intruded.

The strengthening breeze blew a thin wisp of clouds over her nighttime entertainment and made her shiver. Must be rain on the way. She hauled herself up and shone her flashlight beam on her watch. After midnight. All work and no play were making Slate dull and Rose lonely. She stood and stepped carefully on the rocks, up toward the path to the house, where Slate's tall form was silhouetted in the yellow glow of the gaslight in the kitchen. He stood with his back to her, phone pressed to his ear.

Rose grinned wickedly. It was just too tempting. She'd creep up behind him, press herself against him, slide her hands around to the front of his jeans and try to make him lose his cool on the phone. Just to prove she could.

Childish maybe, but the man made her downright giddy.

She turned off her light, moved soundlessly on the carpet of dead leaves and stepped carefully on the noncreaking side of the porch steps, repressing a silly giggle over the fun of launching a surprise attack.

"I don't know how long I can keep her here, Riley.

After two weeks she's going to want to go back to her own life and we're going to have some trouble.''

Rose froze, every muscle like rock in an instant. Her mouth opened. Closed. She stopped breathing.

Then instinct took over and she moved slowly, carefully back down the step, slid under the high porch floor and crouched among the stacks of cut wood, feeling like her body had been turned to ice.

''I don't think she knows anything, but I…wait a sec.''

She heard the creak of his footsteps over her head as he came out onto the porch. Slow-motion, haunted-house creaking, too loud in the peace of the woods. She started to shake.

''I thought I heard her coming back.'' He laughed humorlessly. ''That would be all I needed. I'm just getting her to trust me. I might be able to get something out of her now, if there is anything. But she's smart. I'll have to be damn careful not to— What…? Do you know them…? Yeah, go ahead, see what they want. Be careful.''

Rose pressed her hand to her mouth, stomach churning with sick shock, terrified she would give herself away by throwing up right underneath him. Half her mind was screaming denial, the other half was laughing at her. What the hell did she think? That Prince Charming would materialize at the train station at exactly the right moment with exactly the hideout she needed? Whisk her away and make sure he became everything she didn't know was missing from her life?

Her body convulsed in a silent sob. Of course. He worked with Gel Man and Broken Nose. They threatened her, he rode in for the rescue on his fabulous white stallion.

Lord. She'd stood there and eaten it up. Devoured it, in fact, in huge hunks like a starving dog. How stupid could she be? How could she have let Slate get past every sensible years-in-the-making defense she'd erected? That was all she had left, and the bastard had ripped it away.

All she had left.

"Riley?" Slate's voice rose to a panicked shout. "Riley!"

She heard him punch off the phone and dial again, mumbling obscenities that shocked her. He paced nervously over her head, his breathing shallow and rapid. "Barker, it's Michael Slater. Riley's being worked over. Two, three guys, he didn't know them. I don't know where he is—check his house first. Yeah, okay. Call me as soon as you hear."

He swore again, slumped to the porch directly over Rose's head, in an agony of tension over his friend.

She looked up, stared at the dark outline of his body through the cracks between the pine boards. Tried to feel something. Sympathy. Rage. Anything.

But all she felt was a huge black void inside her. As if her emotions had finally learned their lesson and locked themselves away. No joy. No love. No happiness. But at least no pain.

And thank God no chance of ever being betrayed again.

MELISSA LAY IN HER BED, wondering how long she could amuse herself counting cracks in the ceiling before she'd have to come to grips with the Awful Truth. Penny had already called several times with fun facts about sociopaths from her research on the Internet, dwelling especially on how impossible it was even for perceptive, intelligent people to tell they were about to become corpses.

So thoughtful of her.

Melissa moved restlessly. Sleep was out of the question. Riley hadn't called, but she knew every fiber of her body would stay tense until he did. Then she'd get tenser. She imagined her muscles contracting to such a violent extent that she'd rip through her clothes like the Incredible Hulk.

What the hell could she say to him when she was still such a mass of conflict and uncertainty? She rolled her eyes. Not that it should make much difference. She'd always been a mass of conflict and uncertainty around him. So what else was new? Just because roughly three minutes after she finally admitted she was in love with him she found out he might want to kill her, why should she let that stress her any more?

The thing that really troubled her was that in spite of Penny's well-meant and chilling advice, Melissa was crazy about Riley and thought Captain Watson had all the charm of a horned lizard.

Great. She rolled over and buried her face in the pillow. Now she was doing super well. Now she was using her hormones instead of her brain. *A wise choice, Melissa. Way to go.*

The phone rang. She started, then kept her face in the pillow, not even trying to breathe, since she was pretty damn sure she couldn't, even with the benefit of available oxygen.

It was happening. He was calling. She'd have to chat, talk to the man she loved who might or might not be planning to waste her, and then she'd have to call Captain Lizard Watson and betray him. Because if Riley was a violent psycho, it wasn't a very good idea to ask him for his side of the story.

Forget it. She couldn't do it. She wasn't up to this. Even pickpockets terrified her. How could she make nice with someone who might kill for the heck of it?

The phone rang again. She swallowed. What if she didn't answer and he got worried and came over to check on her?

She gave a choked yell of panic, flung back the covers and lunged for the phone. "Hello?"

"Melissa, thank God you're home. It's Rose."

Not Riley. Melissa's legs buckled; she sank onto the floor and leaned back against the bed, holding the phone to her ear with hands that shook with relief. "Rose."

"I'm desperate. I can't reach a friend of mine. His line is busy and I can't be sure how long I can talk safely." Her words tumbled out in a rough, rushed whisper. "Amanda's not home, either, and I didn't want to leave a message on her tape. You're the only other person I trust."

Melissa nodded wearily. Sure. Trust. Easy to come by. "Where are you?"

"In Maine. I've been kidnapped. I want you to call this friend of mine and tell him where I am."

Kidnapped? "Rose, you should call 9-1-1."

"No. It's his word against mine. I came willingly at first, before I realized. He'd tell the police I'm hysterical or mad at him or something—I can't take that chance. This guy could convince you your name was wrong."

Melissa winced. "Actually, I know what you mean."

"My friend will believe me. He'll send help. Can you do this? Please?"

Melissa let her head bonk wearily against the bed, uncomfortably aware that Captain Watson had instructed her to pass on any information she got concerning Rose. If Melissa agreed to help, she'd be honor bound to do it. Which meant she'd be betraying Rose's trust. But if she *didn't* pass along whatever she found out, she could be obstructing justice.

She let out a huge, painful sigh. Whatever happened to easy decisions, like what should I wear today? Or is it okay or not to put cheese on seafood pasta?

"Please. You're my only hope."

Melissa struggled to her feet. Rose's weakness for men had finally gotten her in serious trouble. Amazing it hadn't happened sooner. But the poor woman did sound genuinely desperate. How could Melissa ignore a personal appeal from someone who might be in danger? She couldn't. Especially because right about now she could too easily see their positions reversed.

Okay. But after this was over she was moving to a Buddhist commune to spend the rest of her life in quiet meditation.

"Yes. Sure. I'll do what I can."

"Oh, Melissa, thanks *so* much. Hurry and write this down. I'm not absolutely certain of the directions, but this is close."

Melissa fumbled on her nightstand for pen and paper and jotted down Rose's whispered directions and the phone number of her friend.

"Okay. Got it. I'll call right—"

Rose gave a sudden gasp. "I think he's coming back." The line clicked off.

Oh, geez. Melissa dialed the number Rose had given her as quickly as her shaky fingers would let her. What the hell was she going to say? *Hi, um, you don't know me but your friend has been kidnapped, and...*

The line clicked, then a busy signal sounded. She sighed, hung up, paced the room for a few minutes and tried again. Still busy. This was insane. This was getting to be like As Melissa's World Turns. She couldn't take much more. But she had to help Rose. If it really had been Rose on the phone. If she really had been kidnapped. If Rose really was her name. If the sky really was blue and the sun would keep coming up every day. How could you be sure of anything?

Melissa dialed the number a third time and froze, startled, when it rang. A deep male voice with a foreign accent answered. Probably another of Rose's Royal Majesties. Melissa took a deep breath and explained the situation succinctly, trying to sound rational and calm.

There was a long silence.

"I'm...sorry for her trouble. Truly. But unfortunately, my energies are all engaged at the moment. Please tell Miss Rose I wish her well."

Click.

Melissa stared at the receiver in her hand, unable to believe anyone could respond to a desperate plea for help as if he'd been unable to attend an impromptu dinner party. With friends like that, Rose was probably better off kidnapped.

Unfortunately, his response left all rescue efforts

squarely on Melissa's totally inadequate shoulders. Which left her only one option: Captain Watson, Lizard Man.

She dialed his cell phone number, lip curled in distaste. Maybe it was just his strangely colored eyes, but the guy gave her the creeps. Which put her in contact with supreme irony, not trusting this man because of his eye color and longing for Riley even though he could be sitting at his house right now, planning to strangle her.

"Watson here." His voice was thick with sleep.

"It's Melissa Rogers. Rose just called me. She was kidnapped. She wasn't sure of the directions, but…she told me where she is."

Captain Watson gave a bloodthirsty shout of triumph that did nothing to make Melissa feel better. She read the directions numbly over the phone; he repeated them back, practically salivating in his eagerness.

"Fabulous. I'll get on it right away. You did the right thing coming to me."

Melissa hung up and sank back on the bed, trying to agree with him. She did do the right thing, didn't she? Of course. How many times had she read a book or watched TV or a movie and wanted to scream at the characters, *Don't go up to investigate the ominous noise in the attic when someone is stalking you, you idiot. Call the police!* Well, she'd done that. Followed her own advice. Put matters that concerned the law into the law's hands.

She stood and moved to the window, parted the curtains and looked out at the enviably peaceful nighttime view of Concord Street. She needed to relax.

Maybe take a shower. A long, soothing stand in nice warm water.

Then maybe she could wash away the overwhelming feeling that she should have called Riley instead.

RILEY WORKED HIS HANDS, trying to loosen the ropes restraining him, as he'd been trying for God knew how long. He moved the wrong way and the pain shot through him again, made him yell behind the tape on his mouth and hang his head, teeth clenched, panting. He was pretty sure he had a lump the size of Kansas on his head. Pretty sure his nose was not a lovely sight. Pretty sure he'd not feel like dancing for at least a week or two.

Allston's men. Had to be. Three of them, very determined, had called him a double-crosser. They must have found out something. That he was working with the FBI? That he hadn't been meeting Rose? Was Watson onto him? Riley couldn't think clearly. Everything confused him.

Melissa.

He moved in an agony of impatience and grimaced at the wave of dizzy nausea that washed over him. He had to warn her. In case Watson found her. In case they thought she knew something. He had to.

A rat peered cautiously at him from the semidarkness of the warehouse he'd been investigating for an insurance fraud case. His phone lay under some shelving, where he'd shoved it when they jumped him. Had to get to it before the battery died. Or before the men came back and *he* died.

Hey, rodent. Hand me my phone. The rat scampered off.

Riley closed his eyes and worked the ropes. Worked the ropes. Worked the ropes...

His eyes shot open. Some give, a slight loosening. He worked his hands harder, ignored the pain, the chafing skin.

Melissa.

He was free.

He tore off the tape; untied the rest of the ropes; slowly, painfully, rubbed some circulation back into his limbs. Dragged himself over to the metal shelves, sat leaning against them and grabbed the phone, grunting from the effort.

Thank God, the battery still worked. He struggled to dial. Damn phone pad had too many numbers; he had too many fingers. Must have a concussion. He'd been in and out a few times already.

Busy. He searched for the redial button and managed to nail it.

Busy. What the hell was she doing on the phone at this hour?

His hands shook over the keypad; his head whirled. *Answer, damn it.*

Busy again.

He felt like crying. Why didn't she get off the phone? He was going to pass out. He could feel it coming, like a hungry black hole, sucking him closer. He had to reach her, had to warn her, had to...he had to...

He opened his eyes with a jolt. Had he been out? For how long?

Melissa.

Call her. One more time. He got the redial button on the second try. The phone rang. Rang. Rang. No answer. Her machine picked up. He waited impatiently, fighting off the blackness.

Please leave a message after the beep. Beeeep.

"Melissa." He put his hand to his head. *Steady. Steady. Just get through the message.* He had to hang on, tell her about the men, about Watson, keep her safe.

The blackness entered his head and turned into white swirling patterns.

"Be careful... Don't let men in... Watson... Don't want you...hurt."

He felt the phone slip out of his hands, felt his lips forming a curse, then slid slowly down and let the black hole take him.

13

MELISSA STOOD, still wrapped in a towel, staring at the blinking light on her answering machine. Who had left a message? And how long ago? She'd been in the shower forever, then had watched some late night TV without bothering to dress. Rose again? Her parents? Penny?

She bit her lip, face twisted in an uncomfortable combination of dismay and hope.

…Riley?

She stepped forward carefully, as if someone might have planted land mines under her carpet, and pushed the playback button.

Click. Whir.

Riley's voice came over the tape, hoarse and barely recognizable. *Be careful…*

Melissa gasped and stepped back. That was it. He was going to kill her.

Don't let men in…

She shook her head, tears of terror springing to her eyes. He was warning her. She shouldn't have let him in, shouldn't have started something with a stranger. She was dead.

Watson…

Melissa stopped a sob in its tracks and stared at the machine. Watson? What— How did Riley—

Don't want you…hurt.

Concern in his voice…and pain. Had something awful happened to him? Was he injured? She couldn't bear to think of him suffering. She couldn't bear that she might be abandoning him when he needed her. She couldn't bear that because of Watson she was too afraid to try and find out where Riley was, to see if he needed help.

The machine clicked. Beeped four times to show the message was complete. Clicked again.

Silence.

Melissa sprang forward and rewound the tape for a fraction of a second. *Don't want you…hurt.*

He was warning her about something, or someone. Watson?

Or himself?

Maybe he hated who he was, hated that he wanted to hurt her. Maybe he was warning her to keep her safe. Penny said some killers wanted to be caught; they hated what they were compelled to do.

Maybe.

Or Watson. She liked that version a lot better. If Watson was the crooked one, then Riley would be warning her against doing exactly what she'd done. Betraying Riley. Betraying Rose.

She closed her eyes and clutched the towel in tight fists against her chest. How was she supposed to know what was true? She found herself wanting to call Bill, to explain this whole horrible situation and get his always rational, detached, emotion-free take, delivered in his trademark monotone. He'd comfort her, chide her gently, give her solid, caring advice. Except he wouldn't be able to get past the part where she'd wanted to have a no-strings fling. Why would she want to do something so out of character? That didn't sound like the Melissa *he* knew. He could have *told* her there'd be trouble.

Don't want you...hurt.

Riley. The ache came on hard and strong. Such tenderness in that weak, strained voice. As if he really cared for her underneath it all. She wanted to weep, but the tears came out in frustrated painful drops, not easy rolling relief.

How was she supposed to know what was true?

She dropped the towel and went over to her dresser, pulled out underwear, a bra, a T-shirt and shorts, not really sure what she wanted to do, only knowing her restless body craved action, not sleep.

She dressed, walked to her front door and peered out, still undecided. Rose's door beckoned across the hall. The riotous red room. The place where everything had started.

Melissa slipped back into her apartment and retrieved the key from her panty hose drawer, went into the hall with quick quiet steps and opened Rose's door.

Streetlight spilled in from outside, illuminating the garish paint to a dark brick color. Melissa flicked on a floor lamp with a muted red shade. A warm pink light lit up the room, making it look more like a bordello than it already did.

She walked through, touching now-familiar objects, remembering the excitement, the passion. How had her fantasy become such a nightmare?

She patted the tin-can giraffe, its nose, its painted aluminum body. Randstetler had been in the news recently, for chaining himself to the fence of a cosmetic company that tested on animals.

Weird sculpture. Weird guy. Weird world. She

moved toward the window and bumped the giraffe's nose with her elbow. The animal teetered despite her clumsy attempts to right it, and tipped forward with a horrible metallic crash to rest flat on its tinny nose. One can popped out of its rear and rolled toward her in a funny, haphazard way, as if it had a weight inside.

Strange. She picked the can up. This one wasn't neatly painted like the others; color had been smeared on in large sloppy swatches. Very messy. You could even see the label through the yellow. Melissa squinted. *B-E-E-F...*

Her eyebrows shot up. *Beefarini?* Randstetler used a can a cow had died for? Not likely. She peered more closely. The top, instead of being neatly welded shut like the others, had been taped and crudely painted over. She shook the can gently, not surprised at the faint thud inside. Had Rose hidden something in there? Drugs? Jewelry? Whatever it was, unless they could get Randstetler to fix it, the future value of the sculpture was—

Melissa's heart skipped a beat. Riley. Going through Rose's drawers. Searching the apartment. Was this what he'd been after?

She tore off the tape, gently pried open the lid and withdrew a tiny bundle, carefully wrapped in cotton and gauze. What the hell? Heart pounding, feeling like a kid playing pirate at the beach who'd actually dug up some treasure, she undid the wrapping. And caught her breath.

A stunning miniature portrait, its frame laden with colorful precious stones—diamonds, emeralds and rubies in a fabulous glittering pattern. The familiar, but strangely aged features of Queen Elizabeth I stared sternly, as if chiding Melissa for allowing the monarch of England to be so closely associated with a giraffe's privates.

Melissa stroked the tiny jewels, gently brushed the glass surface. Exquisite. This must be the Hilliard portrait Penny's cop brother was—

A noise sounded behind her. A swish. Like air being displaced by a moving object. Like the door to Rose's apartment being pushed gently open.

Oh God, hadn't she closed it completely? Melissa's breath ratcheted up into her chest; the blood began draining from her head. She shoved Queen Elizabeth into her shirt pocket, turned and gave a short, choked scream.

Riley.

Looking like someone had run into him with a truck. Blood stained his upper lip and shirt in an ugly swath, as if it had been pouring out of his nose; his left eye was puffy and bruised, his right cheek purple and swollen. Red rings of raw skin circled his wrists, as if he'd been brutally bound.

"I'm sorry, I didn't mean to scare you." The voice was the same hoarse rasp that haunted her on her answering machine. He came forward clumsily, as if it hurt him to move, squinting in the soft light of the apartment, his good eye concentrating hard on her, but in and out of focus, as if he couldn't quite control it, as if he weren't quite himself.

She stood her ground, a seashell rushing noise in her ears, not sure if she was brave or paralyzed by fear, not sure whether to run to him or far away.

"Thank God you're okay." He put a hand to his head as if it pained him to speak. "I was afraid they'd come after you."

Who? Her lips formed the word, but she wasn't sure sound had actually come out.

"Allston's men." He lowered himself into Rose's burgundy wing chair with a grunt that made Melissa wince. "They were annoyed with me."

"Oh." Who was Allston? She didn't know. And if this was what he did when he was annoyed, she didn't want to know. All she cared about was that Riley was hurt, and that getting him medical help meant getting him out of here and into a public setting where she could feel safe while she tried to understand what was going on.

"Riley, you should go to the hospital. I'll call an ambulance." She moved by him to get to the phone.

"No." His hand clamped onto her wrist. She cried out and yanked away, holding her hand as if his touch had burned her.

Riley lifted his head. With an obvious effort, he focused on her face.

"My God, Melissa." His voice sank to an incredulous whisper. "You're afraid of me."

She stared back, unable to explain, to confess her horrible fear, to admit what she'd been told and how far she'd gone toward believing it.

"Is it the face? Does this scare you?"

She nodded. That much at least was the truth. The idea that thugs had attacked Riley, that they'd beaten him, that he could have died made her sick with horror. Worse, he appeared to view this shocking violence as all in a day's work. How could anyone ever get used to that?

He stared at her with a measuring look, as if he were trying to read her mind, to find out how much she knew. "That's not all. There's something else. What is it? What's happened?"

She gripped the arm of Rose's rocker and reminded herself to breathe, afraid she was going to faint in front of him.

"Watson." The name came out under a weight of tremendous contempt. "What did he tell you?"

How did he know? She opened her mouth and emitted a strangled croak. How could she tell him? What could she say? What would he do if she told him?

"Melissa."

God help her.

"He said you're a sociopath." The words came out in a flat, lifeless stream, as if she were responding to a question with her name, rank and serial number. "That you seduce women and kill them."

His face crumpled into incredulity. "And you *believed* him?"

A tear rolled down Melissa's cheek. This hurt. All of it. Everything she thought, everything she said, how he looked, how he looked at her... She was a mass of raw, overstimulated nerve endings. He deserved an answer, an explanation, but she couldn't say a thing that wouldn't hurt them both more. So she stood there and waited.

He shook his head. "You want me to deny it, don't you. Reassure you. Tell you 'Don't worry, Melissa honey, I'm not a serial killer.'"

She bit back a sob. "That would be nice."

"What's the point?" He gestured wearily, but managed to keep his gaze steady. "Aren't sociopaths supposed to be consummate liars? You think you'd know whether I was telling the truth? No way, Melissa. We serial killers are pros. You'll never know until you wake up one morning with my hands around your throat. Right? Isn't that the way you see it?''

"Riley..." Her voice shook, like a little girl getting a scolding.

"Go ahead and make the call if you want." He gestured disgustedly at the phone. "But not an ambulance, just a cab. At worst I cracked a rib, probably have a concussion.''

"Riley..."

"Call, Melissa. Or use my phone. I'm hurting.''

Melissa went to Rose's phone while he dragged himself into the bathroom and turned on the water in the sink. Every instinct had been screaming at her not to trust Watson, not to believe what he told her. She hadn't listened. Hadn't listened to her own heart, her own feelings. Her world, her values, her expectations had been turned inside out and become practically unrecognizable.

She fumbled over the keypad and stuttered to the taxi dispatcher, exhausted, overwhelmed, wanting only to crawl into bed and make everything go away. Sleep for a day or two and try to regain some perspective.

Except she wasn't sure even that would work.

Riley emerged from Rose's bathroom. Melissa replaced the receiver carefully, as if everything she touched was as close to breaking as she was.

"They said ten minutes.''

Riley nodded, sat back in the chair and leaned against the lace antimacassar, eyes closed. Even with the blood and dirt gone, he looked like a beaten warrior who'd popped in for a brief out-of-place visit to civilization. It came home to her suddenly and finally that for all their former intimacy, he was a stranger. He'd always be a stranger.

She sank onto the edge of the rocker opposite and watched him, too heavy with despair to stay on her feet, not realizing until that second how she'd still held out hope some miracle could make things possible for them.

But they couldn't leave it like this. Something had to be said. At the very least she needed to hear his side.

"Why were you investigating Rose?"

"Watson asked me to." Riley didn't open his eyes, spoke without emotion. "He suspected she had valuable evidence the Feds need to link a Massachusetts VIP with Allston. Evidence that started this case as a gift from crime boss to politician with major strings attached, in the form of political favors."

The portrait. "Why didn't Watson get his own detectives to find the evidence?"

"Because there was a leak to Allston in the force." Riley's good eye opened. Even coming out of that wreck of a face, his gaze was compelling, drew her numb heart to him. "Guess who that leak turned out to be?"

"Watson." She knew before Riley even finished his sentence. She'd probably always known.

"His word against mine, Melissa. That's all I'll give you."

She nodded dumbly, tears coursing down her cheeks. She'd been fighting so long and so hard against this man. Because acknowledging that he wasn't a superhero, or James Bond, or a fabulously horrifying deviant, acknowledging that he was an ordinary guy with a job to do, meant she had to stop living in a made-for-TV drama and face the truth: she was in love with a man who didn't fit into her life any more than she fit into his.

The tears came harder.

Riley cursed and lifted himself off the chair, knelt at her feet as he had that first night when he thought she was Rose, and slid his hands along her thighs to her waist in a familiar strong grip.

"I'm not going to make your decision for you," he whispered. "But I can't sit here and watch you cry. I'm not going to hurt you, now or ever. When they were working me over, when I came to after they left, all I could think of was you, how I could get to you, how I could protect you, keep you from—"

"Riley." *Oh God, he cared for her.* She touched the strong lines of his jaw with a shaking hand, not believing it was possible to feel any worse until hopelessness cheated her out of the euphoria of the discovery.

She took his hand, brought the portrait out of her pocket and pressed it into his palm. At least she could show him her trust. "I think you'll know what to do with this."

He inhaled sharply, closed his fingers over it, and turned his face away. "Thank you."

"I'm sorry, Riley. This is all so…strange to me. But I know you'll do the right thing by the portrait. Why I know that, I haven't a clue."

He lifted his head and smiled into her eyes until her heart almost cracked. "How long have you had this?"

"About twenty minutes."

"Where was it?"

"In the giraffe's…butt."

He blinked, then a slow grin spread across his handsome, battered face. Melissa broke into a slightly hysterical giggle.

"Do I need to ask what you were doing rooting around a giraffe's butt?"

She gave in to more crazy, painful laughter. "It was an accident. I knocked the statue over."

"Rose will be devastated."

Rose. Melissa's giggles died. She put a hand to her churning stomach. "Oh, Riley. Rose called me. She said someone kidnapped her. She gave me directions—she wasn't sure they were right. I didn't know what to do...so I called Watson."

Riley swore softly. "When was this?"

"A few hours ago." Melissa slumped in the rocker. How many lives could she screw up in one evening?

"Did you happen to tell Watson she wasn't sure of the directions?"

Melissa nodded.

"Good." Riley fumbled for the phone in his pocket and dialed, his fingers swollen and clumsy over the tiny buttons. He had a brief conversation with someone named Ted Barker, signaled for paper and scrawled wobbly notes on the pink pad Melissa moved to the table next to him.

"Okay." He punched his unit off and put a hand to his temple, his complexion going a shade grayer. "Go to your place and call Watson back. Tell him Rose just phoned with new directions. Give him these. I have to get downstairs for that cab."

Melissa clutched the pink paper and nodded. She should go with him. Make sure he was okay. She couldn't let him leave like this, knowing they wouldn't be together again. "I'll come with you."

"No." He struggled to his feet. "They'll put me to bed and watch me. Nothing you can do. Stay here. Call Watson. Get some sleep. You can come see me in the morning."

She stared at him miserably. He moved toward her, slid his arms around her and held her gingerly against his injured body. She could barely breathe, barely think. She didn't belong in these arms anymore. She had no right to be in them when she didn't intend to stay there.

He pulled back, took her chin in his hand. "This means it's over, Melissa. My part in this investigation. We'll get Rose back, the Feds will get Allston, it's all over. Now you and I can start."

She bit her lip, looked down at her bare feet. How the hell could you reject a man who'd been through such hell?

"Melissa." He backed up against the doorjamb and rested his forehead on his hands, as if holding up his head was suddenly too much effort. "Something tells me I'm about to get hit harder than anything those guys could throw."

"You should go get your cab, Riley. We can talk about this when you're feeling—"

"No." His voice rose and he winced. "Tell me now."

"Riley, for God's sake, look at you. You're a wreck, you need a doctor. Who knows when you slept last, what horrible places you've been. You've had criminals pummeling you all evening. This is not the time to—"

"That's it, isn't it?" He lifted his head, his normal eye dark with frustration. "It's my job. I saw it in your face at the hospital when I told you what I do."

Melissa shook her head, letting her eyes plead with him. *Please, Riley, not now.*

"You still can't give up on that suffocating ideal you've programmed yourself to want." His voice came out hoarse and strained. "Can't give up on your dreary deskbound Prince Charming."

"That's who I am." She tried to speak gently and firmly, but the words came out cracked and shaky.

"Oh, really? What about the Melissa that wants to go around the world? Dress in black leather and explore physical pleasure for the hell of it?"

"She was just a tiny part of me. An experiment, an adventure." She gestured helplessly. "I'm not happy in her skin."

Riley pressed his temples as if he were afraid his head would burst. "Same house, same job, same routine day after day with Business School Bob until you can't tell whether you're living this year or last year, and your whole life just slips away. Is that what you want?"

Melissa gritted her teeth. "Maybe it sounds dull to you, Jonny Quest, but at least I won't have to wait up every night for the knock on the door so I can see whether it's you or the mob or the police. Whether you're in handcuffs or in the hospital or in the morgue. At least Business School Bob can come home after a tough day and talk honestly about what he's doing."

She paced back and forth in short, jerky laps. "What the hell do I know about the world you operate in? I don't *want* to know about that world. I want to be surrounded by honesty. I want trust. I want optimism and touches of idealism. I want normal people being decent to each other. Maybe you think I'm living in a happy-mouse theme park. Maybe I am. But so are most people, and we like it here. Just because there's ugliness in the world doesn't mean I want to invite it into my house. You and I are from different planets, we want different things. It just wouldn't work.''

He let her finish, then stood watching her until she started to fidget. However hard she told herself to stand still and take it, the power from his gaze was too strong, made her feel as if he'd caught her in a lie when she knew she was finally in direct contact with the truth.

He moved away from the door, walked to her and took her wrists, pinned them behind her and brought her close, kissed her slowly and thoroughly, the way he had in her apartment two nights ago. His mouth was warm, sure and achingly familiar; he smelled like himself and, somewhat absurdly, like Rose's pink floral soap.

Melissa turned her head away. ''Don't do that.''

''Why?''

''Because it's not fair.''

''Not fair?'' He moved her closer, until their bodies came together, then planted a line of soft kisses across her forehead. ''Why, because it reminds you that you have feelings for me?''

''Lust doesn't count.''

He kissed her again, a sweet gentle kiss that made a volcano of emotion erupt through her body. ''Does that feel like lust? Was it lust that kept you wanting me on top of you, inside you, the old-fashioned way you were so scornful of?''

''Riley…''

''Let me make love to you, Melissa. Not tonight—

I can barely stay conscious right now. But let me at
least do that. Then you can decide.''

"No." She said the word through a longing so
fierce she could barely stand it. "I can't."

"Why?"

Rose's buzzer sounded, a harsh noise intruding on
their tense whispers, making Melissa jump.

Riley didn't flinch, still gripped her with his hands
and with his stare. "Why?"

"Because…" She shook her head as if it needed
clearing, as if she was still confused, rattled, uncer-
tain. He'd kissed her, that's all. Kisses couldn't
change the facts. Kisses couldn't build a life. They
were only kisses.

The buzzer sounded again, impatiently, twice. She
glanced over at the panel by Rose's door. "Your taxi.
You should get to the hospital."

"Okay." He sighed, released her and stepped back
unsteadily. "I'm going. But not for good, Melissa.
You need time? Take it. But I'm not giving you up
until we at least get the chance to try."

Melissa stepped with him into the hall and watched
his beautiful damaged figure stumble toward the elevator, her heart as bloody and bruised as he was.
She'd done the right thing. It would hurt like hell for
a while, but sooner or later she'd be free of regrets,
happy she hadn't allowed herself to get more entan-
gled in a relationship that couldn't make her truly at
peace, either with him or with herself.

The elevator doors began closing over Riley's
stony, swollen face. Melissa turned away, unable to
handle the devastation of watching him disappear so
completely. She clutched the paper he'd given her and

walked back into her apartment, promising herself to call the hospital every hour to check on his progress.

In the meantime, she had two jobs to do. Number one, practice calling Captain Watson and lying through her teeth. And number two, quell the nagging fear that tonight she might have gotten all the practice she needed—lying to herself.

14

Rose propped the note carefully on her pillow, moved soundlessly into the kitchen and stood next to the back door, ears straining in the blackness for the slightest noise that would indicate Slate might be awake and hear her sneaking through the house. By some miracle, that evening he realized he'd forgotten to go out and pump water. She'd been able to grab his phone and get through to Melissa, pass along Rajid's number and the directions for her rescue.

But when Slate came back into the house and she was faced with the enormity of the acting job ahead, she realized there was no way in hell she could sit here and wait for Rajid to come get her. No way in hell she could disguise hurt this deep. Last night, when Slate was upset and distracted by his friend's trouble, she'd managed to, but not today. Not even Rose was that good.

Best just to leave. Best just to make it seem like she'd gotten bored with him, and sneaked away to avoid a scene. After all, women like her didn't stay with any man too long, right? Women like Rose wanted their relationships easy, carefree and disposable, like frozen meat loaf dinners. She'd find some guy, hitchhike back to Boston, pick up a few things and disappear. Easy as pie. Snap of the fingers. Women like Rose always landed on their feet.

She swallowed to try and ease the sharp sickness in her stomach, then twisted the knob and pulled the door open, hating the fact that noises traveled so clearly through the thin pine walls of the house. Slowly, gently, she pushed open the screen—only so far, to avoid the squeak—and stepped out into freedom and away from betrayal and hurt and love.

Fifteen minutes later the tears hit. She stumbled off the road, instinctively seeking the shelter of the woods, fell onto the soft ground and gave over to the deep wracking sobs, hating the animal sounds she made, the loss of control and the dark tight pain in her chest. She drew her knees up, writhing, gasping for breath, afraid she was going to vomit, literally spew her grief out into the moss.

The sound of a truck and the glow of headlights shocked her into silence. Slate. He'd already discovered her gone. Followed his quarry in his truck like a redneck hunter. She lay as still as possible, her breath coming in high, irregular gasps. A high-powered flashlight beam swung over and past her; the sound of the motor and of tires crunching over pebbles gradually faded. Gone.

Rose jumped to her feet and started running. Ten miles of dirt road. Ten miles to the nearest town, unless she could intercept an early rising lobsterman coming down the point and ask for his help. Of course he would help. Men always helped if you knew how to read them. Knew which ones to flirt with, which ones to plead with, when to play daughter, mother, saint or whore. Rose knew. It was her gift.

She pictured a clean honest fisherman, with a nice family, good business and a healthy fear of God. He'd

help her. But they'd all help her. They always had.
They always would.

Revulsion hit her so strongly she stopped, stunned,
in the middle of the road. The wind whispered overhead, tossing the treetops silhouetted against the
barely lightening sky.

To hell with men. To hell with all of them. To hell
with their needs and their fragile egos and their big
hairy bodies. She'd get to the bus station on her own
two feet. Pay for a ticket and ride back to Boston.
Pick up a few things and hit the road, find somewhere
else to settle. Maybe somewhere like here; she'd
grown to love the Maine coast. A small town where
she could know her neighbors, become part of a com-
munity. She'd get a job, a good one, maybe go back
to school to study writing, support herself. Learn her
lesson from loving Slate, get through the heartbreak
somehow and make the change. Become stronger. Be
her own woman.

A thrill ran through her, right there in the middle
of nowhere in the woods of Maine, and she lifted her
fists into the air and gave a triumphant shout.

Alice Rose Katzenbaum was back for good.

SLATE REACHED ROUTE 1 and turned in a tight circle,
wheels flinging gravel from the shoulder to ping on
the truck's metal underside. *Damn.* When had she
left? What kind of headstart had she gotten? Thank
God the wind had blown branches against his window
and woken him this morning, or he might still be in
bed. Thank God he'd given in to his instinct to check
on Rose, and had found her gone.

He calculated the hours he'd been asleep. Not more
than three. But in three hours she could have gotten

to the highway on foot. Even if she'd left more recently, she might have heard his truck and hidden in the woods as he went by. Ten miles of road, probably five of them dense wood. Needle in the haystack. Hopeless.

Damn.

She also could have gotten a ride with a lobsterman. They were up and around by first light. God knew Rose could get a ride with any man on earth.

Jealousy twisted inside him, until he felt like he'd swallowed barbed wire. As he felt when he'd read that god-awful note and realized she'd left him.

> Dear Slate, I've decided to move on. I'm thinking I shouldn't endanger you anymore in case the people looking for me find me here. You've been more than kind; I've appreciated your patience and your friendship. Maybe we can get together someday when this is all behind us and have a drink and a laugh.
>
> Affectionately,
> Rose

He slammed his hand on the steering wheel. "What the *hell* is this, Rose?" His shout bounced ineffectively around the truck's cab, rang endlessly in his head. *What the hell is this?*

She couldn't know the danger she was in, or if she did she was a fool to ignore it. Assuming Allston's men jumped Riley after discovering Riley had been double-crossing them by cooperating with the Feds and meeting Melissa, they wouldn't stop until they got to Rose. Good as she was, she had no idea how men like that operated, no idea how to stay hidden, cover her trail. She'd go back to Boston and walk straight into their arms. God knew what they'd do to her if they thought she knew where the portrait was.

Slate clenched his teeth and drove faster. After what he'd heard Riley going through over the phone, it didn't bear thinking about.

The road changed to dirt, and he slowed to a crawl and kept a sharp lookout in the woods. Who was he kidding? The fear of the danger, gripping and sharp, was nothing compared to the fear of losing her. How could she leave after what they'd shared? Treat him as if he was just another one of her party dates? She had real feelings for him, he was sure. Not even Rose could fake those.

Maybe he'd been too tough on her, too insistent that she shed her skin. Maybe he'd scared her; maybe he should have taken things even more slowly. But time had been a factor, and keeping their relationship nonsexual until she was ready to let him in completely had taken every ounce of willpower he possessed. Admittedly, he'd been impatient, had probably pressed her too hard to make changes she might not have been ready to make.

His headlights caught movement and the glowing eyes of a fox before it disappeared into the underbrush and left him with a wasted rush of adrenaline. *Damn.*

Rose had seemed so happy, become so natural with him, so different from those first few days. He went over the details of the previous evening for the dozenth time, carefully searched the woods to the right and left with his flashlight, motor humming. He'd been so distracted by worry over Riley that he hadn't noticed anything unusual in her behavior. Now he strained to replay their interactions. Had she displayed any signs of unhappiness? Tension? Given any indication she was thinking of leaving?

No. She'd seemed tired, that was all. Maybe distant, but he'd been distant, too, unable to tell her what was bothering him, and guilty over it. She'd been outside, watching for meteors, when Riley called back—

Slate gripped the steering wheel and swore. He'd been sure he heard a step in the woods, heard her coming back while he was still on the phone. But he hadn't seen her light, and with the wind picking up, he assumed he'd been mistaken. Had she overheard part of his conversation? Assumed the worst when he said he was holding her here?

Sweat broke out on his forehead, under his arms. He had to get to her before Allston's men did. Explain the big picture, make sure she knew he'd been straight with her on everything that mattered.

He sped up, heading for the cottage. He'd call Barker, see if they'd found Riley. Throw his stuff in a bag, close up the house and not stop searching until he found her.

MELISSA ADJUSTED the silver necklace Bill had given her for their first anniversary. He'd like that she was wearing it, and it went beautifully with her new scarlet top. She smiled, and congratulated herself. Her first real smile since Riley had disappeared into the elevator three days before. Three days since Rose's nighttime call, since the tangled mess had finally worked itself out with the good guys on top.

See? She could still smile. Life was okay. She'd taken the day off work, gone clothes shopping, and she had a date with Bill tonight. Apparently the New Ms. Perfect hadn't been so perfect, after all, and he'd called Melissa, saying he missed her.

Ha! She couldn't help being happy about Bill's troubled romance. He was a wonderful man. She could do a lot worse than Bill. After all their years together, all the good times they'd had, they deserved to give it another try. They could probably make it work. Take the old established patterns and give them a little kick into something new, something fresh and satisfying.

Riley's image appeared immediately in her brain, where it seemed to have attempted to cement itself. She smiled at it, a little less naturally this time, and gently pushed it away. No. This was her Getting-Over-Him period. She leaned forward and softened the line of eye pencil under her right eye. Her hand seemed unsteady and she had to swallow a hard lump of threatening tears.

Okay, so Getting Over Him was going to be a bitch. She'd never pretended otherwise. But grief wouldn't kill her. It just needed getting through. She'd done the right thing, made the right choice about who she was and what she wanted.

The door buzzer rang; she glanced at her watch and rolled her eyes, smiling. Five after six. Bill was always exactly five minutes late.

She walked to the door, calmer now, and feeling safe and glad he was here. It would be so great to see him. She'd feel so…so…

She opened the door. Bill stood there, blond-haired, blue-eyed, not too tall. Solid and undistinguished, grinning shyly under a new mustache, offering an enormous bouquet of white carnations.

So…nothing. *Oh, hell.*

"Hi, Melissa." His eyes swept her up and down. "Wow. You look different."

She gestured him in, accepted the carnations and a kiss on the cheek. Okay, safe and calm and glad was still better than thugs and gangsters and beaten bodies. "You like it?"

"It's okay." He shrugged. "But you know me. I'm not much for changes. Speaking of which, I made reservations at La Cucina. I asked for our usual table."

Melissa's body contracted in a wince over which she had no control; she hurried to put the carnations in water. *Take charge, Melissa. Make the changes small at first.* "Bill, why don't we try somewhere new?"

He blinked. "Why?"

"I don't know, I just think it would be fun to make a change. You know, a fresh start. Get out of the old ruts and make some new ones."

She winced again and fussed over the carnations, which stuck stiffly out of the widest vase she had. Even new ruts were still ruts. Maybe she should have waited to see Bill until Riley's presence dimmed from her memory a bit more, so the comparisons wouldn't be so apparent. So she wouldn't feel as if her future held only certain suffocation from routine and predictability.

Why was she doing this?

"Okay, sure. We can go somewhere else. Some night soon, we'll do that."

"Great." She gave the carnations a final, rather vicious pat and took his arm. "It's really good to see you, Bill."

He turned and kissed her warmly. She closed her eyes and concentrated on the soft wetness of his mouth under the scratchy mustache, concentrated again on how nice it was to feel calm and safe and glad, so she wouldn't compare him to Riley. Because this *was* what she wanted. Right?

Double hell.

"Mmm, nice." He lifted his head and grinned down at her. "Let's go."

"I have a better idea." She pressed against him, full of desperate hope. "Let's not. Let's blow off the reservations and go to the Publick House for a beer and free hors d'oeuvres. Then let's go dancing. Then let's come back here and order in pizza and watch a sexy movie."

"Wow." He did a pretend double take. "That's quite an offer."

"And?"

"Well..." He fidgeted. "It's just that we have a reservation. They're expecting us."

"So?" She tipped her head back and quirked an eyebrow, trying to stave off the inevitable letdown. "Let's do something unexpected."

Bill frowned and examined her minutely. "Something's happened. You're not the same."

"Don't be silly." She stepped away from him in alarm. "I'm exactly the same. Why would I have changed?"

"I don't know, Melissa. You tell me." He frowned harder, examined her more minutely. "You've been with another man, haven't you?"

Melissa gasped; her eyes shot wide-open. Was it that obvious? "I...well, I...it was nothing."

He put his hands to his hips, which meant he was upset and trying to hide it. "I don't think so."

"What..." Melissa cleared her throat to try and bring her voice down to its usual register. "What makes you say that?"

"He changed you. He couldn't do that if it was nothing."

"No." Melissa shook her head emphatically and stabbed herself in the chest with her thumb. She had to make sure he was very clear on this. That *she* was very clear on this. Because if it wasn't very, totally, absolutely clear to both of them, then she might have made the most stupendous mistake of her life. Which, after seeing how she reacted to Bill and how he reacted to her, was starting to seem like a distinct possibility. "*I* changed me, Bill. I tried to be something I'm not, and it didn't fit."

His eyes flicked miserably over her outfit. "I wouldn't be so sure about that. You seem to wear it pretty well."

"Bill—" She bit her lip. What the hell could she say? How could she begin to tell him what had happened since they last spoke?

"I'm not surprised, actually."

Melissa put her hands on her hips, which meant she was upset and not at all trying to hide it. "What do you mean?"

"You've always had this wild streak in you."

Her mouth dropped. Of all the things he could have said... "Wild? Me?"

"You always wanted more. More things, more places, more people...more sex. I never felt like I was enough for you. That's why I was sort of...rigid in response." He hunched his shoulders and looked down. "I've been in a ton of therapy over all this. You're pretty intimidating."

"Me?" Melissa repeated with a gasp, her brain refusing to supply any other response. "Intimidating? Bill, I'm the most plain ordinary woman on the planet."

The minute the words came out of her mouth she realized what she'd said. She did feel like the most plain ordinary woman on the planet. Around Bill. Around Riley she felt enticing, witty, alive and free, albeit a bit confused sometimes. Why had it taken her this long to figure it out?

"No way, Melissa." Bill shook his head emphatically. "No way. You're amazing. It was a mistake to think I could come back. You need someone more like you, someone who lives closer to the edge than I do."

She stared at Bill, heat flooding her face, unable to believe what she was hearing and feeling, and how right it all sounded and how right it all felt. "Why did you stay with me for so long?"

"Because." He rubbed the back of his neck and eyed her sheepishly. "I wanted to feel like I was that kind of person. But I'm not. Not even remotely."

"Oh, Bill." She melted toward him; he enveloped her in a solid, comforting embrace.

"So, who is this guy?" His voice came out cracked and strained.

She sighed against his shoulder. "A private detective."

"Kind of like *Spenser for Hire?*"

"Yeah." She smiled up at him, trying not to look as dreamy as she felt. "Kind of like that."

"Oh." He nodded resignedly. "He sounds perfect for you."

She tried to speak, but the tears got there first, sliding two warm trails down her cheeks.

"You know..." She shook her head and laughed a little. "I think he is."

RILEY RUBBED the sandpaper around the last flowing curve of the lion's mane, traced the same path with his fingers and smiled in satisfaction. There. Smooth as satin. He picked up a tiny chisel and began carefully carving the lines that would make the mane textured and lifelike. A mirror would go in the middle and the whole thing would sit on top of the dresser he'd made, so when Leo looked in it, his little face would be reflected in the center of the lion's head, as if he were the magnificent beast himself.

Riley had worked steadily, obsessively on the piece for the past two days, since the idea had come to him and he'd been feeling well enough to try. He still had occasional headaches, his body still protested movement in certain directions, but he was definitely on the mend.

If only he could say the same for his mood. He'd stayed away from Melissa as promised, given her time to think things over, come to some decision regarding their relationship. But he hated the helpless, unfamiliar feeling of having his fate in someone else's hands. Detested the vulnerability, the inactivity, the pain. Mooning around like some whipped, pathetic Romeo.

He loved her. And she could hurt him like nothing had ever hurt him before.

His phone rang. He put down the chisel and went

to answer, trying to suppress the rush of hope that it might be Melissa.

"Slate here." Slate's voice sounded edgy, nervous, totally unlike his usual tone, nonchalant even under enemy fire.

Riley raised an eyebrow. "What's up? Where are you?"

"I've been staking out Rose's place. Barker just called. They found her visiting her mom out in Framingham. They're putting her on a train back here."

Riley pressed his lips together to keep back the laughter Slate wouldn't understand. What a pair. Gemini—the invincible fighting unit that helped keep foreign countries safe for democracy, helped the FBI shatter Allston's criminal empire and bring a crooked senator to his knees—reduced to a quivering helpless mess by a couple of women.

"What are you going to do?"

"Go meet her train, what else? Wish me luck."

"You don't need luck, Slate."

"No?" He laughed humorlessly. "What do I need?"

"Balls."

Slate laughed again, a short anxious burst. The sound of traffic came over the line, swishing through streets made wet by a late night downpour.

"Riley."

Riley tensed. There was something else. Something he wasn't going to like. "Yeah?"

"Melissa just went into her building." Slate cleared his throat. "With some guy."

Riley's body reacted with a flood of primal jealousy that left him speechless.

"Does she have a brother...or something?"

"No." He punched off the phone, moved toward the stairs, took them two at a time.

Of course, there might be a perfectly logical explanation. Maybe they were old friends, having a late, friendly chat in her apartment. Riley grabbed his keys, flung open the door and stalked out into the rain, down the steps, onto the sidewalk, broke into a run.

Or maybe she was trying to get rid of his memory by becoming involved with someone she thought was more appropriate. Maybe she'd already found Business School Bob.

Tough. If she thought Riley would just sit there and let another man touch her, she had some serious rethinking to do.

He jammed his car into gear and sped through the wet city streets toward Cambridge.

His phone rang again.

"It's Slate. You still home or on your way to do something stupid?"

"On my way."

"Good." Slate chuckled. "Because if you weren't, I was going to remind you about the balls."

"Don't worry, I've got 'em."

He said goodbye, turned off the phone and veered around a corner, splashing an unlucky pedestrian. He had them, all right.

And he'd be damned if he was going to let the woman he loved cut them off.

15

ROSE KISSED HER MOTHER, straightened the limp figure gently in her wheelchair. Her mom made a strange guttural sound, lifted her head and fixed Rose with wide, blue, childlike eyes.

"Goodbye, Mom. I'll come again soon."

Her mom's head dropped down onto her chest, bobbed up again and dropped down.

The nurse smiled and patted Rose's shoulder. "Have a safe trip. We'll take good care of her."

Rose nodded and thanked her. At the door, she turned back, something she never did. She hated leaving, hated the sight of her mom looking so blank and so horribly alone.

She glanced over at her mom's roommate, in a similar stage of Alzheimer's. The woman's husband was with her, as he was every time Rose came to visit, reading to her, playing her music, wiping her face gently and with such love. He'd bring flowers, greet her like his favorite daughter, call her sweetheart, nestle next to her and tell her about his day.

Rose glanced back at her mom, slumped and silent in her chair, one last time before she left to get her train.

TWO HOURS LATER, she sat staring at the raindrops on the windows, spattered, running together, dripping down and onto the gray metal sides of the car. Ten minutes until they arrived at South Station. It was still hard to believe the whole nightmarish month was over—beginning with the break-in at her apartment and ending with the Feds intercepting her on her way in to see her mom yesterday. The thieves had been looking for something Senator Mason had hidden in the giraffe sculpture; someone named Allston had sent the thugs to the train station; Ted's TV Repair was the cops keeping an eye on her; and Slate...Slate had been trying to protect her.

She leaned her head against the cool glass of the window. She'd already cried her eyes out in her hotel room last night. Not one of her strange fits, but real, honest, grieving tears that stopped when her emotions ran dry and left her peaceful, if still bereft.

She'd have to see him again, of course. He'd come find her, probably soon. She couldn't afford rent *and* hotel space, and she was tired of hiding, anyway. The next move she made would be a positive step to her new life, not just running away from her old one.

The train jerked unpleasantly over merging tracks as they approached the station. Seeing Slate would be awful and wonderful and thrilling and exhausting. Rose had had enough of that kind of upheaval for a while. That small town somewhere in New England beckoned, wonderful and thrilling all on its own, by virtue of the quiet, self-reliant existence she could fashion there.

Rose closed her eyes and sighed. Her feelings for Slate sat like a heavy dull pain in her chest, interfering with the anticipation of the future she knew she wanted, that she deserved.

The train came to a halt at the station; passengers scrambled to disembark. Rose picked up her bags and joined the stream of people, trying to blot out memories of the last time she'd been here.

The crowd filed past the glass doors into the station; Rose kept her gaze firmly fixed on the back of the business suit in front of her. She wouldn't look around. She wouldn't remember. She wouldn't hope or expect or dream anything. She'd look straight ahead and think straight ahead and walk straight ahead into the new life she was making.

She crossed the large room, went down the steps into the subway, swiped her monthly pass, lunged at the turnstile with her hip and gave a grunt of pain. Damn thing was stuck. She swiped her card again, pushed harder. It didn't budge. She sighed, backed up to try another one. The handle of her bag caught on the metal rod and she jerked back clumsily.

"Need help?"

Rose caught her breath. Slate stepped into view and leaned across her to disentangle her bag. The movement brought his body close, close enough that his scent reached her and her skin shivered with the need to touch him.

"No, thanks." Rose pushed the desire away, her brain a whirl of confusion and uncertainty, and freed her purse herself. "I got it."

He fixed her with a keen glance, his blue eyes piercing and magnetic despite weary circles and a slightly anxious cast. He gestured her through another turnstile and fell into step beside her. "The Feds weren't too hard on you, I hope."

"No, they were fine." She stopped and turned, desperately glad to see him. "It seems you were rescuing me, after all."

He put down a small shopping bag he'd been carrying, grinned and raked his hands through his short hair. "So it seems."

"Well…" She shrugged, helpless to express everything she had to say to this man who had no right to look so solid and male and damned fabulously irresistible just when she'd decided how terrifically her life would go on without him. "Thank you."

He moved so quickly she didn't have a chance to protest—pulled her toward him and kissed her, hard and passionately on the mouth, held her tight against him so that her body flashed into flame.

She tried to pull back, but he held her still, kissed her again, over and over, the passion he'd always denied her twice as potent and powerful as she'd imagined it so many times. A train roared into the station, blowing dust and hot air around them, took on and let off passengers, roared away.

Finally he stopped, leaving her limp and breathless, crazed and giddy and barely able to stand on her own feet. God, she'd missed him. And one sight of him was enough to make her little town in New England already feel as lonely as her mom in the nursing home.

"I have something for you, Alice Rose." He picked up the bag he'd been carrying and handed it to her. She rummaged in the tissue paper with shaky fingers and came up with a slender pottery vase, glazed in earthy blue-and-green tones, with tiny ferns imprinted on the side.

"It's for the shelves at the cottage. I thought we could start new, start putting a lifetime of our own memories up there." He crossed his arms over his chest, hands shoved into his armpits. "If that's what you want."

She stared at him, aching with love and tenderness, aching to give him the answer he wanted, to take the terrible, uncharacteristic vulnerability away from his eyes. But she couldn't do this to please him. She had to please herself, too.

"Slate." She fingered the delicate design on the vase. She wanted him. She wanted to believe she could be with him and retain the sense of self he'd pushed so hard to give her. But she also wanted time to be alone with Alice Rose Katzenbaum, to get to know her again and live life through her. "I need to be independent for a while. Find my way by myself."

"Of course. I understand." He glanced at his watch. "Ten or twenty minutes long enough?"

She laughed in spite of herself. "I was thinking in terms of years."

"Nope." He shook his head, trying a grin under those serious eyes. "Too long."

"Months?"

He drew her to him and kissed her again. "I'm not going to crush you, Rose. I want you to be independent, I want you to be free, to choose your own life. I just want to be part of it."

"I want that, too." She clutched the vase to her

heart, amazed at how easily the words were spoken, how true they were. "But not right away. Please understand."

He pinned her with a frustrated, sexy blue stare, lips tightened, jaw clenched.

"Okay." He nodded. "We'll go slow. I'm patient. We can have dinner tomorrow night. Then you can take a night off. Then the next day we can get married."

She laughed, then smiled up into his eyes, let him see the love she felt for him. "I'm determined on this one, Slate."

He groaned and clutched his temples. "Okay, okay. I know when I'm beat. You want to wait, we can wait. Cut me off at the knees, put the chain around my neck. I'm yours, I love you, and I'll wait as long as it takes."

Rose flung her arms around him and kissed him with her entire soul. "Six months. Just give me six months to be me, on my own. Then you can have me."

"Mmm." He ran his hands up and down her body. "All of you? Forever? Only for me?"

She nodded and drew a slow X across her chest, making the childlike gesture the solemn oath she knew in her heart it was.

"All of me, Slate. Forever. Only for you."

MELISSA WAVED TO BILL and closed the door with a sigh of relief. She thought he'd never leave. They'd had a nice evening; she'd always love Bill in a friendly, peaceful way. The way she always thought you were supposed to feel toward your husband. The way she'd never in a million years settle for now.

She rushed to the phone and dialed Riley's number, heart pounding with excitement and a touch of terror. Busy. She made a face and put the phone down. Paced for a minute. Called again.

Busy.

Okay, she could make herself crazy doing this. She popped in the tape of *The Philadelphia Story* and sank onto the couch, vowing to wait at least ten minutes before she tried again. The movie was one of her all-time romantic favorites. Katherine Hepburn, resisting the fabulous fireworks sparked by her ex-husband, Cary Grant, flirting with the solid, earnest reporter played by Jimmy Stewart, before realizing her one true love, the one she would always belong to, was the thrilling man she'd never stopped loving.

Duh.

Melissa grinned and reached for the phone again in a fit of impatience. How could she ever have thought going back to Bill was a good idea?

She'd given in. Surrendered to the glorious possibility that she'd found a true soul mate, a man she could feel passionately about for the rest of her life. One who would take all sides of her—wild, sedate, ordinary, extraordinary—and cherish every one.

She dialed his number, clutched the phone and closed her eyes. Ringing. Ringing.

Her eyes opened. She frowned. Strange. She could hear a phone ringing through her wall.

"Riley here." His voice seemed to come from the

phone *and* from her hallway. Someone pounded hard at her door.

Melissa stood, adrenaline pumping, still holding the phone to her ear, and walked toward the knocking.

"Slate? Hello? Who the hell is this?" His voice came through the phone, brusque and hoarse.

She disconnected the line, opened the door and sucked in her breath. He stood there, eyes on fire in the dim hallway. Rain had dampened his T-shirt and hair, left glistening drops on his skin. He smelled of the summer night and every fantasy male she'd ever imagined.

"Riley." The word emerged charged with love and joy and everything she could possibly feel.

"Where is he?" He spoke with a quiet ferocity that took her completely aback.

"He?" She stared at him blankly. "You mean Bill? How did you know—"

Riley took two steps into the apartment and closed the door gently behind him, without taking those intense, angry eyes from her face. Every movement showed deliberate control, but the impact of his emotion was like physical violence. Melissa shivered, unabashedly thrilled by his jealousy and power.

"Was he here tonight? With you?"

"We had dinner. He's a friend. Nothing more." She almost laughed at how true it was, and held up the phone. "That was me calling you. The second he left. I couldn't dial fast enough."

The anger in his eyes began fading, replaced by a guarded look. "What did you have to say to me?"

"That…I want to be with you."

"Now?"

"Yes."

"With toys?"

She shook her head.

"An experiment?" He took a step toward her. "For fun?"

"For real." Her voice shook. "Forever, if that's how it turns out."

He held her eyes for a breathless moment, then pushed his phone slowly back into his pocket and pointed to hers, eyes dark and hungry. "Put that down."

She set it on a nearby end table, barely resisting the urge to fling it over her shoulder. He lunged forward, swept her into his arms and carried her into her bedroom as he had before, except this time she wasn't fighting herself; this time she was at peace.

If she could call having her body on fire with love and lust being at peace.

He laid her on the bed, pulled his T-shirt over his head and lay next to her, his body warm and solid beside her. He swept his hand over the material across her stomach, pulled it up to expose her skin, slid his hand to her breasts. "I've never seen you wear red, except that underwear I brought. Did you buy this for him?"

"I thought so." Her voice came out a soft gasp; his fingers were warm and sure, caressing her through the thin lace of her bra. "But now I realize it was a warning. One he recognized before I did."

Riley pulled the blouse up and over her head, tossed it onto the floor behind him, unhooked her bra, slid it off her shoulders and sent it spinning after. "A warning?"

She looped her arms around his neck and pulled him to her. "That I'm not the woman he knew before. That I belong to someone else."

"Damn right." He lowered himself onto her and kissed her. "If he'd been here I would have shot first, asked questions later."

"Romantic, but messy."

"That's me." He grinned, rolled them both to one side and slid her pants down and off, then her panties, taking his time, making her crazy with impatience, with longing for the full lengths of their bodies to come together.

His hand followed the intimate line of her leg from her ankle, up and over to her inner thigh, then pushed between her legs. Desire hit her, hard and wild; she kept her legs closed and rocked against his forearm, slid her hands down and undid his jeans—the button, the zipper. Pushed the material down and away, freeing his erection to her exploring fingers.

He let her touch him briefly, keeping his arm strong between her clenched legs, giving in to sexy sounds of pleasure that echoed hers. Then he took his jeans the rest of the way off and slid on top of her, wrapped his arms around her, holding her to him as if he wanted to bring her inside his own body, making her feel loved and protected and horny as hell all at once.

"Oh, Melissa," he whispered. "You feel so damn good."

She swallowed, teary and thick-throated from happiness; stroked up and down his back, savoring the smooth, muscled feel of his skin, the rough brush of chest hair against her breasts. He pushed slowly, rhythmically, his erection hard and teasing against her sex until she thought she'd go crazy wanting him inside her.

"Riley." She opened her legs eagerly, reached down for him, guided him to her wet center.

"Wait." He held back.

"Why?" She tried again, panting with frustration. He resisted. "Melissa."

"What?"

He lifted up on one elbow. "I just wanted to know if this old-fashioned sex is boring you yet."

She gaped for a startled second, then burst into laughter at his mischievous grin. "Oh, Riley. I love you."

The mischief left him; he leaned down and kissed her, lowered his body tightly against hers, pushed inside her and lay still. Melissa closed her eyes, wanting to capture the feeling forever, the thud of their hearts next to each other, the absolute intimacy of their joining, the hot, huge sensation of being filled by him.

Then he began to move and she lost everything. Everything but Riley, and the spiraling certainty that she was headed to oblivion, that nothing would ever be as good as this, the total connection, the joining, the exchange of their bodies and passion and hearts.

Her climax grew slowly, spread over her, rushed her into a long moment of burning ecstasy. She clasped Riley hard, rocked up against him, felt him come inside her, heard him whisper her name, his body tense and pulsing with hers. Tears mingled with her cries, mingled with the sensations and emotions so far beyond anything she'd ever felt.

Then slowly, inevitably, she came down, not regretting the slide back into consciousness when reality held their future together.

He lifted his head, kissed her sweetly, gently. She responded with her whole self, no longer afraid, no longer holding back.

"I love you, too, Melissa."

She sighed, a tremendous gooey sigh of happiness that made him smile. He kissed her again, rolled to his back and brought her with him, nestled her tightly against him. "And I think I could stand to do that again sometime."

She laughed and wrapped her leg over him. "Like when?"

He glanced at his watch. "How about I pencil you in after I save the world from evil?"

"That would be fine. As long as it doesn't take more than an hour."

He came up on his side and traced her lips gently with his thumb. "Melissa, I don't want to give up my job. I love what I do. It fits me."

"I know. I wish I loved mine half that much." She gazed up at him earnestly. "I wouldn't ask you to quit. It will be hard on me at times, I won't lie about that, but I'm willing to try if it means—"

He held up a finger to stop her. "However. I am prepared to take some time off, on one condition."

She raised an eyebrow, surprised by his offer. "What's that?"

"You come on a trip with me around the world."

"What?" She struggled to sit up. "Are you serious?"

He looked her straight in the eye. "Deadly."

"You mean quit my job?"

"The one you don't love."

"And just…leave?"

"Yup." He pulled her back down next to him and stroked her breasts, her stomach and down between her legs until she felt herself getting hot all over again. "What do you say?"

She laughed from sheer excitement. What *could* she say? Why the hell not? Go on an adventure and come home to a new life and a new outlook. With Riley beside her. She locked her arms around his neck and pulled him onto her. "I'd say it sounds a lot like you—too good to resist."

He grinned and pushed the hair gently off her forehead. "I wanted to make your fantasy come true."

"Oh, Riley." She reached up and kissed him, reached down and touched him, felt his body respond, felt her heart swell to bursting with love and happiness. "Believe me, you already did."

CALL THE ONES YOU LOVE OVER THE HOLIDAYS!

Save $25 off future book purchases when you buy any four Harlequin® or Silhouette® books in October, November and December 2001,

PLUS

receive a phone card good for 15 minutes of long-distance calls to anyone you want in North America!

WHAT AN INCREDIBLE DEAL!

Just fill out this form and attach 4 proofs of purchase (cash register receipts) from October, November and December 2001 books, and Harlequin Books will send you a coupon booklet worth a total savings of $25 off future purchases of Harlequin® and Silhouette® books, AND a 15-minute phone card to call the ones you love, anywhere in North America.

Please send this form, along with your cash register receipts as proofs of purchase, to:
In the USA: Harlequin Books, P.O. Box 9057, Buffalo, NY 14269-9057
In Canada: Harlequin Books, P.O. Box 622, Fort Erie, Ontario L2A 5X3
Cash register receipts must be dated no later than December 31, 2001.
Limit of 1 coupon booklet and phone card per household.
Please allow 4-6 weeks for delivery.

I accept your offer! Please send me my coupon booklet and a 15-minute phone card:

Name: _____

Address: _____ City: _____

State/Prov.: _____ Zip/Postal Code: _____

Account Number (if available): _____

---

097 KJB DAGL
PHQ4012

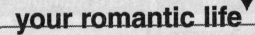

WITH HARLEQUIN AND SILHOUETTE

There's a romance to fit your every mood.

Passion

Harlequin Temptation

Harlequin Presents

Silhouette Desire

Pure Romance

Harlequin Romance

Silhouette Romance

Home & Family

Harlequin
American Romance

Silhouette
Special Edition

A Longer Story With More

Harlequin
Superromance

Suspense & Adventure

Harlequin Intrigue

Silhouette Intimate Moments

Humor

Harlequin Duets

Historical

Harlequin Historicals

Special Releases

Other great
romances
to explore

$\mathcal{H}$ugh Blake,
soon to become stepfather to
the Maitland clan, has produced three
high-performing offspring of his own. But
at the rate they're going, they're never going to
make him a grandpa!

There's *Suzanne*, a work-obsessed CEO whose Christmas spirit
could use a little topping up....

And *Thomas*, a lawyer whose ability to hold on to the woman
he loves is evaporating by the minute....

And *Diane*, a teacher so dedicated to her teenage students she
hasn't noticed she's put her own life on hold.

But there's a Christmas wake-up call in store
for the Blake siblings. Love *and* Christmas miracles
are in store for all three!

Maitland Maternity Christmas

A collection from three of Harlequin's favorite authors

Muriel Jensen
Judy Christenberry
&Tina Leonard

Look for it in November 2001.

Celebrate the season with

Midnight Clear

A holiday anthology featuring
a classic Christmas story from
New York Times bestselling author

Debbie Macomber

Plus a brand-new *Morgan's Mercenaries* story
from *USA Today* bestselling author

Lindsay McKenna

And a brand-new *Twins on the Doorstep* story
from national bestselling author

Stella Bagwell

Available at your favorite retail outlets in November 2001!

Silhouette®

Where love comes alive™

Visit Silhouette at www.eHarlequin.com

PSMC